I0609569

harmless secrets

A HARMLESS WORLD NOVEL

HARMLESS TROUBLE
BOOK ONE

MELISSA SCHROEDER

EDITED BY
NOEL VARNER

HARMLESS PUBLISHING

contents

Also by Melissa Schroeder   v

Hawaiian Terms   xvii

Chapter 1   1

Chapter 2   11

Chapter 3   23

Chapter 4   33

Chapter 5   45

Chapter 6   55

Chapter 7   67

Chapter 8   75

Chapter 9   83

Chapter 10   91

Chapter 11   103

Chapter 12   115

Chapter 13   125

Chapter 14   141

Chapter 15   155

Chapter 16   165

Chapter 17   179

Chapter 18   189

Chapter 19   197

Chapter 20   209

Chapter 21   219

Epilogue   231

Harmless Revenge   239
TFH TEAM BRAVO   241
About the Author   245

also by melissa schroeder

THE HARMLESS WORLD

The Original Harmless Five

- A Little Harmless Sex
- A Little Harmless Pleasure
- A Little Harmless Obsession
- A Little Harmless Lie
- A Little Harmless Addiction

Rough 'n Ready

- Rough Submission
- Rough Fascination
- Rough Fantasy
- Rough Ride

Harmless Trouble

- Harmless Secrets
- Harmless Revenge
- Harmless Scandals

The Wulf Family

- Faith
- Taboo
- Trust

A Little Harmless Military Romance

- Infatuation
- Possession
- Surrender

Task Force Hawaii

- Seductive Reasoning
- Hostile Desires
- Constant Craving
- Tangled Passions
- Wicked Temptations
- Twisted Emotions

TFH Team Bravo

- Justified Secrets-coming soon

THE CAMOS AND CUPCAKES WORLD

Camos and Cupcakes

- Delicious
- Luscious
- Scrumptious

The Fillmore Siblings

- Hate to Love You
- Love to Hate You

Juniper Springs

- Wild Love
- Crazy Love
- Last Love
- Imperfect Love

THE SANTINI WORLD

The Santinis

- Leonardo
- Marco
- Gianni
- Vicente
- A Santini Christmas
- A Santini in Love
- Falling for a Santini
- One Night with a Santini
- A Santini Takes the Fall
- A Santini's Heart
- Loving a Santini

Semper Fi Marines

- Tease Me
- Tempt Me
- Touch Me

The Fitzpatricks

- Chances Are

THE MELISSA SCHROEDER INSTALOVE COLLECTION

Dominion Rockstar Romance

- Undeniable
- Unpredictable
- Unexpected
- Tempted

Mafia Sisters

- Stealing Destiny
- Guarding Fable

Faking It

- Faking it with my Billionaire Boss
- Faking it with my Brother's Best Friend
- Faking it with my Frenemy

The Fighting Sullivans

- Falling for the General's Daughter
- Falling for the Girl Next Door
- Falling for my Best Friend
- Falling for my Baby Mama

Also Included

- Kiss my Tinsel
- Dad Bod Rockstar

Texas Temptations

- Conquering India
- Delilah's Downfall

Hawaiian Holidays

- Mele Kalikimaka, Baby
- Sex on the Beach
- Getting Lei'd

Once Upon an Accident

- The Accidental Countess
- Lessons in Seduction
- The Spy Who Loved Her

The Cursed Clan

- Callum
- Angus
- Logan
- Fletcher
- Anice

The Sweet Shoppe

- Tempting Prudence
- Cowboy Up
- Her Wicked Warrior

By Blood

- Desire by Blood
- Seduction by Blood

Hands On

- The Hired Hand
- Hands on Training

Telepathic Cravings

- Voices Carry
- Lost in Emotion
- Hard Habit to Break

Bounty Hunters, Inc

- For Love or Honor
- Sinner's Delight

Saints and Sinners

- Seducing the Saint

- Hunting Mila

Lonestar Wolf Pack

- Primal Instincts

Texas Heat

- Scorched

Spies, Lies, and Alibis

- The Boss

SINGLE TITLES

- A Calculated Seduction
- Chasing Luck
- Going for Eight
- Grace Under Pressure
- Operation Love

- Saving Thea
- Snowbound Seduction
- Sweet Patience
- The Last Detail
- The Seduction of Widow McEwan

To the Harmless Addicts. Without you, there never would have been ten years of Harmless and there definitely wouldn't have been a tenth Harmless Book.

hawaiian terms

Aloha - Hello, goodbye, love
Bra-Bro
Bruddah- brother, term of endearment
Haole-Newcomer to the islands
Howzit - How is it going?
Kama'āina-Local to the islands
Mahalo-Thank you
Malasadas- A Portuguese donut without a hole which started out as a tradition for Shrove (Fat) Tuesday. They are deep fried, dipped in sugar or cinnamon and sugar. In other words, it is a decadent treat every person must try when they go to Hawaii. If you do not try it, you fail. Do yourself a favor. Go to Leonard's and buy one. You are welcome.
Pupule - crazy
Slippahs - slippers, AKA sandals

Devon Stryker followed his sister through the stalls at Pike Place and tossed his brother-in-law a nasty look. Micah just smiled as he jostled Alana from one shoulder to the other. His niece giggled. Her beautiful blue eyes danced with happiness as she waved at him. Devon forced himself to smile for her, but once she turned around, he scowled again.

"I can't believe I let her drag me down here on a Saturday," Devon muttered.

The amount of tourists and locals was always bad on a Saturday. Being considered one of the place to hit on the waterfront for tourists always made it kind of a madhouse. Today, it was worse. It was one on of those perfect sunny days with mild temperatures and not a cloud in the sky. That meant there was a sea of people rolling through the popular waterfront market. It was something Devon always tried to avoid. He really hated people in general, but add in a tourist attraction, he was ready to punch the next person who asked him for directions.

Micah strode through the crowd, his gaze taking in the multitude of people as if he didn't have a care in the world. Devon knew better. Micah always knew where Dee was and who was around him. Still, Devon kept a keen eye on the little cap his sister wore. It was bright red and easy to see. If he didn't keep his gaze on it, he knew they would lose her.

"You're the one who mentioned it would be fun," Micah said. The amusement in this tone was unmistakable.

Being reminded of his stupidity didn't make Devon feel any better. He turned to say something to Micah, but an annoying middle-aged man barreled between them. Devon ground his teeth and tried not to growl.

"No. I said *she* would have fun. Not *we*. That girl never did listen to me."

Micah chuckled. "She listened. She just chose to ignore you."

"As her husband, you're the one who is supposed to control her. Isn't that what your lifestyle is about?"

"That's not the way I like to control her."

Devon shook his head as he continued to follow Dee through the market. He would have never picked a man like Micah for Dee. He was part owner of a BDSM club in Hawaii and came from a rough background. Still, the Native American Dom had turned into a devoted husband and father. A brother couldn't find fault with a man who clearly worshiped the ground Dee walked on.

"Ugh, that's not something I wanted to think about."

"Then you shouldn't have brought it up, son."

Pushing those thoughts aside, Devon hurried on to catch up to Dee and find out just where she was going.

"Hey, lady, slow down. Where are you going?" he asked.

Dee turned to face him. She looked different than when he'd found her. Her blonde hair was now back to her natural brunette, and she had a roundness to her only a mother could claim. And she was happy. So freaking happy that she was smiling up at him when he felt like screaming.

"I heard about this place over here for lunch. I wanted to see if they had seats."

He glanced at Micah, who stepped up beside him. "Might as well give in, Dev. She's only going to complain if we don't go."

"And it is only going to get worse as this pregnancy progresses," Devon said. "She blackmails us to do what she wants."

Micah shrugged. "I'm happy to be blackmailed by my beautiful bride."

Dee laughed. "And that's why I love you, Mr. Ross."

She leaned up on her tiptoes and gave Micah a kiss, then kissed Alana on the cheek.

"Just face it, Devon, you're stuck down here for the day. Make the most of it." Then she kissed him on the cheek. "And if you complain again, I promise to call you every time I have a craving for Hawaiian ice."

That was a very real threat. His sister had gone through some wicked cravings during her last trimester with Alana, not to mention the mood swings. He didn't want to be anywhere in sight when that happened.

He nodded. "Let's go."

He turned to follow her again and that's when he heard it. A lyrical laugh, a bit rusty, and still as seductive. It was as sweet as it was sultry and it sunk beneath his flesh. It was one that he had heard only once or twice years ago. He knew it was her, knew she was there. He scanned the crowd around him as everything—noises and people—dissolved away. Devon walked away from Dee and her family as he sought out the woman who still haunted his dreams.

The crush of people seemed to grow, as he tried his best to move toward the sound. He pushed against a few people, ignoring the curses and the dirty looks. Devon growled in frustration. He knew exactly where the sound had originated, but now, he couldn't seem to get there. It was as if a wall of people had been erected to keep him away. Adrenaline coursed through his veins as he kept his gaze focused on that same area.

Then, in a split instant, he saw her. At first, he wasn't sure it was her. Her hair was longer and darker, and she was dressed down. It had been over four years so he knew there was a chance he was imagining the connection. Then, she turned enough so he could see the curve of her jaw. Watching her walk, he knew it was her.

It was the woman he had been fantasizing about for four years.

"Ali," he yelled, trying to gain her attention, but the sound of the crowd drowned him out.

He continued to yell her name as he drew closer and closer. Then...she turned. Just a quick second and her gaze landed on him. Her eyes seemed unfocused, then, her attention landed on him. Her eyes widened as she stared at him. In that splint instant, Devon knew she had seen him. His breath tangled in his throat as their gazes locked in those few seconds. Someone walked between them and Ali turned away from him. He cursed and started to fight against the crowd. It only took a few minutes for Devon to realize he had lost her.

He stopped running. He spun around and around, trying to see if she had doubled back. Frustration coiled in his gut as he shoved a hand through his hair.

Micah came striding through the crowd. The people seemed to move out of his way subconsciously, as if they knew he was a Dom. It might also be because Micah walked as if he were still on the hunt for a fugitive.

"Where's Dee and her MiniMe?"

"They're getting us a table. Dee said she would wait a total of ten minutes before ordering her food. After that, we were SOL." He looked around at the crowd then turned his focus completely on Devon. He could see himself in the mirrored sunglasses his brother-in-law favored. "What was that all about?"

Devon sighed. How did he explain the mind jolting experience he just had? He'd never told a soul about Ali, about their night together. He'd kept it a secret, his only, little secret that he hadn't wanted to share with anyone. The fact that he had been that close to her after all this time left him frustrated. Devon thought it was hard to accept the fact he couldn't find her. Now that he had seen her, the need for her clawed at his gut.

So fucking close.

"Devon?" Micah asked.

He looked at his brother-in-law. Concern stamped Micah's features. It was out of character for him to run through a crowd yelling a woman's name, so Devon kind of understood. He didn't really want to explain himself, but he knew Micah wouldn't let it go.

Devon smiled. "A woman."

Micah chuckled and clapped him on the shoulder. "It always is. Can you see her anymore?"

Devon shook his head. But he would. He knew where she was, at least for now.

Micah's phone buzzed with a text. He looked at it and laughed again. "Your sister says to hurry."

"Does she?"

"Yes, although she used much more colorful language."

"All right," Devon said as he turned away from his quest for now.

"So, this woman?"

Damn. Since Micah had married Dee, he had gotten a really bad reputation for meddling in his friends' lives. The one thing Devon did not need was his brother-in-law trying to fix things.

"What about her?" Devon asked.

"Is this anyone I know?"

Devon shook his head. "I haven't seen her in years."

"But you chased her down in the market?"

He glanced at Micah, who was looking straight ahead. "Let it go."

"Oh, I'll let it go. Dee is the one you will have to deal with."

Devon stifled another growl. This was going to be one long freaking day.

ALICIA LEANED up against the building down the street from the market and caught her breath. As she pulled in deep breathes of air, her heart pounded against her chest. Her head spun as she felt sweat slide down her back. She held her daughter's hand so tightly she was amazed Bridget hadn't complained. Bloody hell. That had been a close one.

What was Stryker doing here and just how had he found her? She had thought she had been well hidden until today. There she had been, minding her own business and she'd heard her name. Only a handful of people called her by the nickname —but she had recognized his voice. It had excited her at first. Memories of that night had flashed through her head as she turned to scan the crowd for him. Then she had seen him.

And she had run like her bloody life depended on it— because it did.

"Why did we run, Mummy? Who was that man shouting at us?" Bridget asked.

Alicia looked down at her daughter. Her cheeks were ruddy from the quick jaunt through the market and her eyes were sparkling. She was smiling, thinking they had been playing some kind of game. Thank God for that.

As her daughter stared up at her with those big beautiful blue eyes—the ones that looked just like Devon's—she knew she couldn't lie. God knows she wanted to dismiss it, but even at the age of four, her daughter was perceptive. So, she went for a half-truth.

"Nothing, the crowd was just getting to me."

Bridget nodded sagely. Unfortunately, Alicia had invented phobias. She didn't like large crowds, but it had more to do with their safety. Alicia usually avoided them, but when Bridget had asked to go to the waterfront today, it had been hard to resist the request. It was probably one of the last nice weekends before winter really took hold.

So Alicia had given into her daughter and they had been having a brilliant time. As the crowd had grown, she had stifled the need to run away. She did not want to raise a coward. Life was best experienced, or so her father had said— before her mother had been killed. So while she had to keep her safe from the likes of Stryker, Alicia did her best to make sure she experienced something else other than their home.

And today, it had almost been the death of them. It was odd that he had smiled at her the way he did. It wasn't an evil smile of triumph. It had been relief, with a tad bit of that sexy smile she'd seen years ago.

She realized she was standing out on the street leaving both her and Bridget exposed.

"Why don't we head home? We can have an early dinner and then make some popcorn and watch a movie. Your pick."

Bridget smiled and clapped her hands together. "That sounds brilliant. I think we should watch Frozen."

Of course she did. Bridget had been obsessed with the movie since it had come out. But, in this, Alicia couldn't deny her daughter the simple joy of watching her favorite movie. Their jog through the crowded market forgotten, she grabbed Alicia's hand and pulled her toward the parking lot where their car was.

All the while Alicia tried to pretend she hadn't seen that man. It had only been a split second, but she knew it was him. There was that smile he'd given her that night, the one that had made her lose her mind and her morals. She would never forget those amazing blue eyes, not when she saw the same ones every day. She looked down at her daughter. Bridget was the one good thing to come from that terrible time in her life. And for that, she would never regret that night—but it didn't mean she was stupid.

They might have to move again. She hated to do that to Bridget, but there might be no other way.

Their lives could very well depend on it.

two

The loud chatter of restaurant patrons filled the air around them while Dee stared at Devon as if he had lost his mind. She looked at Micah who shrugged, then she turned back to Devon.

"Are you crazy?"

Maybe he was, but he refused to admit it until he was sure.

"So, you spent one night with this woman...how many years ago?" she asked.

The tone of her voice told him everything he needed to know. She was positive he had lost his mind. With their family history, there was always a chance of mental illness, so he really didn't blame her. But she really should know better. Most of their family members were slightly eccentric, and Devon himself had a reputation of being a bit of a recluse among people in his business. That meant a lot in the world of gaming because many of the top designers were reclusive.

"Well, how many years?" Dee asked again. He could tell from her tone she wouldn't let it go.

"A little over four."

She pursed her lips while she handed Alana a sippy cup. "Four years?"

"Yes."

What was Ali doing in Seattle? She had let him assume she lived in the UK when he met her. And why had she looked so freaking scared when she realized who he was? The look on her face had been one of surprise. That he expected. What he didn't expect was the way it had dissolved into terror. There was no way around it. The woman was frightened of him in a way that made her run away. What had happened to her since he'd last seen her?

"Devon!"

He shook his head and tried to focus on his sister and what she was asking.

"What?"

She rolled her eyes and tapped her fingers on the table. "I think we need you to take another IQ test. Your brain cells seem to be melting by the minute."

He glanced at Micah, who had his head down in the menu, but Devon knew he was laughing. For a long moment, he looked out the window, studying the way the sun danced over the waves. The Ferris wheel continued to turn and people went about their own daily lives. It was as if something Earth shattering hadn't happened.

"Devon!"

He turned and looked at his sister.

"What were you asking?" he asked.

"The woman."

"Oh, yeah, Ali. Well, about four years. Actually, when is your anniversary again?"

Dee's eyes narrowed, but Micah saved Devon by rattling off the date.

"So, yeah, right around then."

Again, she pursed her lips. That was never a good thing. Dee had a devious mind.

"And you are sure you saw her in the market? Amongst all those people?"

He nodded. "Without a doubt."

"A one night stand and you're still obsessed with her?" Dee asked.

"Love, I would search every continent looking for you after our first time together," Micah said, taking her hand and kissing her fingers.

"You're so sweet," she said smiling.

"You are both disgusting," Devon said. "I had an emergency and had to leave."

Micah was studying him and he nodded. "You left her when you went to kidnap Dee."

Devon sighed. "I didn't kidnap my sister."

"Yeah, you kind of did," Dee said with a laugh. "But are you sure it was her?"

He shifted in the booth as the waitress brought them their drinks. Once she left, Dee pressed on with her interrogation.

"What makes you think it was her?"

"I know it was her."

"Why are you so positive?"

He didn't want to answer, but from the determined look on his sister's face, he wouldn't be able to avoid the questions. He looked at Micah, who now had taken an interest in the conversation. Dammit. Now he felt like a fool, but Dee would never let it go.

"I heard her laugh."

Dee said nothing. Micah nodded as if he understood.

"And you say this was definitely her. Why are you so obsessed with her?" Dee asked.

He shrugged. "I have no idea. I just am."

Micah took pity on him. "Leave him be, Dee. If he says he saw her and if he is obsessed with her, well, let's not talk about it any longer. The less we know, the less we can help the prosecution when the time comes."

Dee wasn't happy about it, but she listened to her husband and they ordered their food.

Long after Bridget and Alicia had finished the popcorn and Elsa had sung her last note, Alicia sat in bed with her daughter sleeping beside her as she searched for information on Devon.

She had kept an eye on him over the years. The fact that he was probably the one sent to distract her while her father was attacked had made it a priority. Sure she had gone to look for him. With his name popping up in her father's notes, he had been her only lead. When everything had fallen apart, what she was supposed to think.

After a property search in his name, she found nothing. He still lived in Las Vegas, but he apparently split time between there and Honolulu. There was a credit card trail that had him in both places.

And now he was in Seattle. Bloody hell.

Staring at the screen, she continued to wrap her hair around her finger. This was not a good development. Something was tickling the back of her throat. Panic. It was bloody panic. She did not panic. She was a Hughes.

Buck up, Ali girl.

"Easy for you to say, old man," she murmured, a small smile curving her lips. She could almost hear her father chuckle at the familiar banter.

Her smile faded. Alicia had grown fond of Seattle. Her house in the woods had become a sanctuary. Safety. Even her cousin Millicent had no idea where she lived, and she was the one person Alicia trusted. It was better for both their sakes that Alicia kept her in the dark.

With a sigh, she closed her laptop. There was only so much she could find out in any one sitting. If she lingered in her search, it would raise red flags. A man like Devon Stryker would have some kind of security to cover his name.

After brushing her teeth, she slipped back into bed with Bridget. Her daughter rolled over and snuggled against Alicia. All those years ago when she had found out about her pregnancy, she had been shattered. Her father had just died and Alicia had barely escaped an attempt on her life. Then, realizing she was three months late and pregnant had almost broken her.

She brushed a strand of Bridget's golden hair away from

her face. She would do anything to keep her daughter safe... *anything*.

Alicia just hoped she could keep her safe from the man who helped create her.

DEVON SHOVED his hand through his hair and blinked trying to focus on the screen. He stretched up and little sharp pricks of pain filtered out from his spine. When he moved his head from side to side, his neck cracked. Damn, he was getting old.

"You're not still up, are you?" Dee said.

He scowled but didn't look away from his laptop. "I'm sitting here, aren't I?"

She looked at the clock, then at Devon. "Have you even been to bed yet?"

"No," he said, as he continued to go through the security footage from Pike Place. It had taken a few hacks and a call to an old friend to get it, but he had the footage now and he wasn't giving up. He knew he would find Ali.

"Devon."

He didn't look away from the screen. He knew if he did, there was a chance he would miss her. After spending all night looking for her in the footage, Devon refused to give up now.

"Devon." This time she yelled it.

He tore his attention away from the screen to frown at

her. She was still wearing her pajamas and her long hair was all messed up—like she'd just got out of bed.

"What?" he asked, equally as loud.

"Oh, the sound of sibling love in the morning," Micah said, as he came into the kitchen with Alana in his arms. Micah looked at his daughter. "Promise you'll be nicer to your brother or sister when he or she finally arrives."

"It's not my fault. Devon's staring at the screen stalking a woman he says he met four years ago." She slapped him on the back of the head.

"Dammit, Dee."

"Dammit," his niece repeated with a huge toothy grin.

"Oh, nice going, Uncle Dev," Dee said, settling her hands on her hips.

"Sorry," he mumbled as he turned his attention back to the screen. He had no sleep and his temper was always dangerous when he was tired. "Don't hit me again."

"You need help. You're starting to act like Crazy Uncle Shane Noah. Pretty soon, you'll be wandering around the town in your bathrobe."

Devon scowled at his sister, then grabbed his coffee cup. He brought it to his lips before he realized it was empty.

"I don't need help. I don't even own a bathrobe."

She walked over to stand beside him and looked at the screen. "So, it's normal to illegally hack into the security cameras at Pike Place?"

"You said I need help. I don't. Both of us left *normal* a long time ago."

When she didn't say anything, he turned around to apologize, but she was staring at his laptop screen. Her eyes were wide and her face pale.

"How do you get that to go back?"

"Go back?" he asked.

She fluttered her hand at the screen. "Rewind, whatever?"

"Why?" he asked, stepping up beside her.

"I think I saw her. There!" She pointed at the screen. "You were following her, and then she ran. There she is."

He looked toward the screen, but then Dee shook her head. "Oh, wait. She has a kid. That's not her."

Devon couldn't pull his attention away from Alicia or the little girl she had beside her. They had run through the crowd, the little girl's braids flying behind her. Alicia had leaned up against a building to catch her breath. The video was fuzzy, but he knew that was her. She talked to the little girl, as if trying to catch her breath, then they walked, hand in hand, down the street and turned into a parking garage. It was the same one Devon had parked in for the day.

Damn.

"How old would you say that little girl was?" he asked, as he rewound the footage and watched again. He zoomed in, but the picture was fuzzy.

Dee shrugged. "I don't know. Probably about four."

He looked at Dee and her face went blank. "No. You can't know that."

He used the control to rewind the footage again and paused it. "I'm not saying she's mine, she could be someone else's kid. But...it's odd."

"Now you have to find her," Dee said. "You need to at

least know whether or not that little girl is yours. If she is, you'll need to get a lawyer involved, and I can watch the house."

"Hey, you two, don't go making any crazy plans together," Micah warned as he poured some cereal in a bowl for Alana.

"What do you mean by that?" Dee asked, her hands on her hips. "We don't make crazy plans."

"Yeah?" Micah asked.

"Yeah," Devon said. "We never really do anything *that* crazy."

"Let's remember the last time I had to call Carino to help you out of a bind," Micah said.

"That wasn't our fault. Devon didn't know that woman was a fan of his games." She looked at him. "You need to keep your face off of stuff. You're too pretty."

Micah muttered under his breath as he filled a sippy cup. Dee rolled her eyes and faced Devon.

"So, how do we find out where she lives?" she asked.

He played it again and zeroed in on the parking garage. "We just need to find her car. Then we'll know where she lives. We know where she parked, so we can probably find out where she lives."

Maybe he would be able to find out just why the hell she ran away from him. He played the footage back, pausing at the moment she noticed him.

Even in the blurry image, Devon could see the terror that crept over her features. He swallowed as his stomach roiled. There was something really, really wrong. Finding her was the most important thing now. The woman he had spent the night with didn't look like she would back down from anything. But today she had.

Was the girl the reason? Did she have some connection to him, or was it just a weird coincidence? He needed to discover all those secrets.

And, he might just find out why she looked as if she was scared to death of him.

THE MOBILE RANG, bringing the former agent out of a deep sleep.

"Yes?"

"There was a hit. Someone was looking for information on Stryker."

Irritation danced through the agent's blood. "You woke me up for that? There are a lot of people who look for the bastard. Call me—"

"Please. Listen. There was someone checking out the cameras at the Pike Place. It was well hidden, but someone went to a lot of trouble to get information from there. And there was one very important section. I sent you a pic on your secure email."

The agent pulled the laptop from the other side of the bed. After keying in the password, the email popped up. The picture was grainy, but it was no doubt Alicia Hughes. There were more of them, including one with Alicia against a building holding the hand of a little girl.

"This was in Seattle?"

"Yes."

"Do you know where they live?"

"Yes."

"Take care of it."

The agent hung up and smiled. Finally, so close to the end after all these years. One little mistake, and could finally be over with.

three

Two days later, several fractured federal laws, and a few thousand dollars tossed at those who helped, Devon and Dee parked down the street from what he was sure was Ali's house. It was set off from the road and surrounded by trees. Secluded even. It was a rancher, with a long front porch. The grass was trimmed and the flower beds were filled with plenty of colorful flowers that gave it a cheerful look. The warm fuzzy feeling was ruined by the fact the house had enough security to protect her from an invasion from a foreign country.

There were cameras on the roof and more than likely sensors around the area. Flood lights sat atop each corner of the house. And that was just what he could see from the front.

"Well, someone doesn't like visitors," Dee murmured, a thread of admiration in her voice.

He glanced at her and noticed that she was looking up at the roof. Dee never missed much.

"Apparently not."

But he couldn't judge Ali, not when he had the same kind of a security at his various houses. Anyone who had been in the business didn't fuck around with security.

It did appear that someone in the house had a background in some kind of law enforcement. Was she living with a man? Was there even a chance that she was married now… or maybe even then? Did that mean Ali had some kind of connection to him he didn't know about? And what did that mean about their meeting? Was it just a chance encounter or had she picked him out?

He had known the CIA had put a price on him. Of course, it was only good if he was brought in alive. Thanks to Conner Dillon, that was removed about the time his father had been arrested for trying to kill Dee.

"Hey, earth to Dev," Dee said snapping her fingers in front of his face. "Where did you go?"

He shook his head. "I guess we should go knock on the door."

"Let's go," Dee said, but she frowned when he pulled a gun out of the glove box. "There could be a little kid here, Dev."

"And a woman who is afraid of something. With that amount of security, she might see us as a threat. Just being careful and keeping the safety on."

She opened her mouth to argue with him, but years of being her brother had taught him how to deal with Dee. It was best not to even He slipped out of the car and tucked the gun into the waistband of his jeans, then covered it with his jacket. Dee was still frowning at him when they walked up the driveway.

He continued to ignore her and he heard her sigh. She apparently decided to let it go for now. They both stopped when they reached the front walk.

"It looks nice," Dee said. "Well, if you ignore that she apparently has more of a hard-on for security than you do."

And it was nice. The neighborhood was upper middle class from the looks of it and each lot had at least an acre around it. It was a perfect place to raise a kid.

He was on alert for anything as they walked up, but nothing happened. No alarms sounded. Weird. For someone who had this much security, he would have thought they would have triggered some alarm. They knocked on the door. No answer.

Dee shifted her weight from one foot to the other, a clear sign that she was getting impatient. When Dee got impatient, bad things could happen.

"It was too much to hope for that she would be home. She probably has a job or something," Dee said.

She looked in the front windows and Devon walked around the front, looking for clues about the woman who lived there. The name on the mortgage was Francine Williamson, not Ali, but that didn't mean anything. She could have been using an alias that night. It would explain why it was so hard to find her before.

But he knew it was the same woman.

"I think we better go, Dee," he said. Now that he knew where she lived, it would be easier to figure out how to approach her.

Before Dee could respond, a crossover SUV drove up and parked in the driveway. She apparently hadn't seen him or Dee, which was odd considering the security she had around the house. She stepped out of the car.

She was casually dressed in a pair of jeans that hugged her hips. The jacket was more about utility than fashion. His heart jerked, then doubled in speed as he watched her move. No matter what she wore, he knew it was her. No one in the world moved like her. Every motion was fluid, as if she had some kind of soundtrack playing in her head.

He couldn't seem to catch a breath, as if all the air around them had been sucked away. Images of that night washed over him, the sounds of her gasps and moans. He licked his lips and was positive he could taste her there.

"Ali," he said.

She froze, then turned to face him. Her face was pale, her eyes huge and he knew fear when he saw it.

"That's not my name." Her voice was hoarse when she spoke. The English accent was nowhere to be found. She reached behind her.

"Don't." It was only a simple word but she understood the implications. He wouldn't hurt her unless she posed a threat to Dee.

"I've no idea what you're doing here or why you're calling me by that name. If you don't leave, I'll call the police."

Denying her name, what they had together....it pissed him off. Why was she doing this? And why did she look as if he was going to hurt her?

"Yes, it is. I know you. We met in Vegas."

She was shaking her head in denial when he heard small footsteps around the front of the car. A smaller version of Ali stood there, with blonde hair like the night he had met Ali. She had his eyes.

"Mummy, isn't he the man who yelled at us in the market?"

He looked at Ali, his eyes narrowing as he studied her. "Why don't you answer her, Ali?"

"Ali? Mummy says only her father called her that."

Devon said nothing as Ali finally stepped in front of her daughter. "Please leave."

Her voice was tight, not with anger...but deep-rooted fear. It quivered at the end and he knew it wasn't normal for her. She thought he would hurt her? Or did she think he would hurt the child?

"I'm not leaving until I have an explanation." He crossed his arms over his chest.

She straightened her shoulders. "I'll not explain myself to the likes of you."

He opened his mouth to ask just what the hell she meant, when Dee stepped out from behind him before he could stop her. "Hey, there."

Ali's gaze took in Dee, traveling down to her stomach, then she looked at Devon.

"I'm Dee, Devon's sister. And you must be...well, what do you want to be called?"

The little girl peeked out from behind Ali. The smile she offered reminded him of Alana.

"Francine is what people call her here," she offered.

"Then, Francine, and you are?" Dee asked smiling. His sister could get a mute man to talk with that smile of hers.

Ali opened her mouth to probably tell her not to reveal her name, but her daughter was quicker than she was.

"Bridget Williamson."

"That is a fantastic name, if you don't mind me saying. My name is Dee and I have a little girl just a little bit younger than you. Her name is Alana."

"I think we all need to have a nice long chat," Devon said.

Ali looked from him to Dee then back to him. "Is she really your sister? The one who died?"

That answered one question. She knew his true identity. That meant she had known who he was all along.

"Yes."

Dee stepped forward. "I promise I am. You can call my husband if you want an affirmation. He stayed behind to watch my little girl."

Disbelief moved over her features. "But you came out here pregnant. And he let you?"

"Micah said something about Devon and me needing someone to bail us out after you had us arrested for trespassing."

Ali's lips twitched, then she sighed. "Okay, but there are some rules."

Bridget leaned closer to Dee. "Mummy likes rules."

"Mind your manners, young lady." Her words were tinged with a bit of that English accent he loved and the same authoritative tone he'd heard Dee use on many occasions.

Bridget immediately pouted, but Ali paid her no mind. He'd seen his sister do the same thing. Micah and Devon were not immune to Alana's pouts, but Dee didn't put up with it.

Ali pulled out her keys and looked from Dee to Devon. "Bridget, go up on the porch. You two, stay here until I have the door unlocked."

Devon wanted to argue with her, but Dee touched his arm. He looked at her and she shook her head.

"Get rid of the gun, you wanker. You will not bring it into my house," Ali said as she slipped past him. He nodded.

They turned to watch Ali unlock the door, then stand in front of the security pad as she punched in her code.

"Go in, Bridget," Ali said. "Mr. Stryker has something he needs to put in his car."

She never took her gaze from his as she once again ordered him to get rid of his gun. He did her bidding, jogging down the driveway to put the gun in his glove box, then rejoining his sister.

Ali looked from Dee to him. "One wrong word, one thing that sets me off, and you leave."

They both nodded.

"Come on in."

They were walking up the path when Dee said, "Behave yourself."

He frowned but nodded. He would behave if need be so he could find out just what the hell was going on.

ALICIA SENT Bridget to her room to play while she faced off with her unwanted visitors. Devon sat at her kitchen table, a brooding figure. A very sexy, brooding figure.

Lord, where did that thought come from? She was really going mental if she was thinking about him that way. This was the man responsible for her father's death. Even as she thought that, her heartbeat ticked up a beat. It wasn't from fear.

She was a horrible, horrible person. She was surely going to hell. Or at least purgatory.

Dee sat beside him, smiling. Now that she saw them side-by-side, she could see the resemblance. They were twins. She had forgotten that. When she realized she and Devon were in a stare down, she decided to move this along.

Refusing to sit down, Alicia walked across the kitchen floor and leaned against the counter. "I've no idea what you think you're doing, but I'll not have you scaring my daughter."

"Our daughter."

The two words sent a shaft of fear coursing through her blood. "You have no proof."

"Believe me, I can afford a DNA test, but she has my eyes."

She crossed her arms. "You'd have to get a court order before I would let you do that."

Devon's face turned into a mask of anger. He opened his mouth, but his sister interrupted him again.

"Let's worry about that later on, okay? Why don't we start with something easy? Are you Francine or Ali?"

Alicia hesitated. Over the last few years, she had become

good at avoiding direct questions, only skimming the surface of who she really was. Most people didn't really want to know the truth, just the version that made them most comfortable.

She studied Devon, gauging how much she should tell him. It seemed stupid to deny who she was with a man who had biblical knowledge of her body. Instantly, she was thrown back into that night, the sights, the sounds, the way it felt to have his body crush her body into the mattress.

"Alicia. Alicia Hughes."

Devon grunted. "At least you didn't lie about that."

She might have invited him into her house, but she would not put up with that attitude. If he knew her better, he would probably have kept his mouth shut.

"And you were truthful? Running off and leaving me in the bed with a bloody note?"

He opened his mouth to fire off a retort of some sort, but his sister stopped him. Dee groaned and covered her face, then she dropped her hands and scowled at her brother.

"Oh, Devon, you didn't leave her like that, did you? That's horrible. No wonder she doesn't like you. If I had been in the same situation, you would definitely be talking at a higher octave."

Devon scowled right back. "Dee, you don't know the whole story."

"No, I don't. And you left out the part of leaving a note. Have you broken up with women in a text?" She closed her eyes. "No, don't tell me. You probably have. I share DNA with a jerk."

Alicia tried not to smile, but seeing Dee berate Devon

was kind of nice. It had been a long time since anyone had stood up for her.

"Yes, he did. Just a note saying he had an emergency. No number, nothing."

She opened her eyes and looked at Alicia. She saw the twinkle in Dee's eyes. "Oh, wait until I tell Micah."

"Stop, Dee. That's water under the bridge."

Alicia snorted and crossed her arms beneath her breasts.

Devon narrowed his eyes. "What I want to know is when she found out she was pregnant, why didn't she find me?"

She could lie, but she didn't. She did look for him. "You are not an easy man to find."

"That's true," Dee said. "Especially then, when our father wanted to kill us. But that's another story."

Alicia blinked. "Okay."

Devon wasn't happy with that answer. "That doesn't explain why you ran away when I saw you two days ago."

The question brought her back to reality. This wasn't a pleasant exchange between friends. This was a man who had caused her world to dissolve into a pile of crap. Anger wrapped in a thick coat of fear balled up in her stomach.

"Why did I run away?" Alicia asked. Even she heard the slight edge of panic in her tone.

He nodded, acting like he had no idea why she would want to be as far away from him as she could.

"Because you had my father killed and tried to kill me, that's why."

four

"Why don't I help you make some coffee?" Dee asked after a long silence.

Alicia really didn't know what she would have done without Devon's sister there. She looked at the woman and smiled, but she was frowning at Alicia.

"Oh, wait, you probably drink tea."

Alicia shook her head. "No, I've taken up the great American past time."

Dee smiled. "That's good because I can't make a proper cup of tea to save my life. I know English people are very particular about their tea. Americans just can't make it right according to most of the English I know."

Devon said nothing. He just watched her. This was not the sweet, sexy man who had charmed her into bed. This was a stoic stranger who watched her like a predator.

This was the man she expected to find in Las Vegas.

"Just tell me where everything is and I'll take care of it," Dee said.

She directed Dee to the coffee, then she faced off with Devon.

"So, you think I killed your father?" he asked. There was no emotion in his voice, nothing that told her about his feelings. His face was a blank mask without emotions.

"Not directly."

He ground his teeth together. "Explain."

"I am not your subordinate. I don't take orders. And let me remind you, *I* made it through my training."

Anger flashed in the depths of his blue gaze. *Oh, well, you don't like that do you*? Devon had disappeared during his training. For a man like him, it might be a little hard to accept that he had failed. Truthfully, he hadn't completely failed. Devon was definitely competitive. It was something that made him a success in the world of game development. For him to walk away from a challenge like that, there had to have been an incident.

"So, you're with The Company?"

"No. I was with MI-6. I'm not with anyone anymore. Except Bridget."

Another beat of silence. "We will be talking about her later."

She didn't respond to that. She didn't know what to say. Fear and anger still clogged her throat and had her heart was tripping out a vicious beat. There was no doubt in her mind that he was the father of her child. With a test, he could prove the girl was his and with his money and power, the court case for custody would be huge. Alicia knew she was probably as rich as he but she knew that he had more connections in the American legal community.

"So, you came to find me."

"My contact told me my father was looking for you before he disappeared." She shrugged, not liking the way he continued to watch her. He was trying to unnerve her. He was, but she would be damned if she would let him know it.

"And who was your father?" he asked.

She cocked her head to study him. He sounded genuine, but again, he was trained by the CIA. She never trusted spooks, being one herself.

"Sir Walter Hughes."

Again, he said nothing. It was as if he was trying to wrap his mind around the circumstances. "You're royalty?"

She shook her head. "My father had a title because of his service to the crown."

"What did he do?" Dee asked, as she grabbed some cups from the cabinet. Devon frowned and opened his mouth— probably to tell her it wasn't important, but she answered before he could stop her.

"That's classified. I would give you the details now that he's passed, but even I don't know."

"Walter Hughes." Devon muttered, his gaze unfocused. "Where do I know that name from?"

"You and he crossed paths. Had to. It was in his notes I read. You were prominent in them. I saw your name there more than once." Off in the corners, scribbled in her father's handwriting. Whatever her father had been working on, Devon had figured prominently.

"No. No we didn't. He used my name I have now?"

She nodded. Then it hit her. "When you were with the CIA, you had another name."

"The one I was born with, yes, so it can't be anything to do with my research there. But...I do know your father's name."

"Well, bully for you."

His lips twitched. "I collect a lot of information."

Yes he did. She had read his file, knew that his IQ was beyond genius level. The CIA had such high hopes for him. She'd only discovered a small part of his file. Devon's ability to dance in and out of security systems undetected was unnerving. They had wanted to tap that skill and when he disappeared the CIA went into freak out mode. That kind of ability out running around was dangerous. Alicia knew at least one higher up had lost his job for it.

"Yes, well, my father was very interested in you. There was a lot of information on you at his house."

"Why didn't you ask him?"

She sighed. "Because I couldn't find him."

He studied her for a moment, as if trying to discern if she were lying. She wasn't, but even if she was, she doubted Devon would know. She had been trained by the best.

"Your father was missing? Did this happen often?"

"Not that often, but he was in the business also. One thing you learn when you are raised in the business is that sometimes people disappear. But it was odd I couldn't seem to find him at all. We had a few ways of getting in touch, but he never responded."

He drummed his fingers on the table. "So they sent you after me?"

She could lie about that, easily. Devon might under-stand if she had been ordered to find him. But for some reason, she couldn't lie about that. Not now and not to him.

"No. I did that on my own. I was actually on my own without backup when I went looking for you."

He said nothing for a few moments.

"You came to Vegas to approach me—and apparently thought I was dangerous—with no backup?"

His tone told her he thought she was an idiot. She straightened her back.

"I don't think you would understand."

More fingers drumming on the table. "We'll get back to that later. First, we need to talk about our daughter."

Her heart ticked up a bit. "What do you want to know?"

"Why didn't you contact me?"

He was obtuse. She just told him why and he kept asking. "As I said, you are not the easiest person to find."

He waved that away. "But, still, you found me once."

She sat down in the chair opposite of him and sighed. "That morning when you left me, I got another call from my cousin."

"He's in the business too?"

"She, and yes."

He wanted to ask more. She wasn't stupid. The man thrived on information. The thirst for knowledge shimmered just beneath the surface. He might be good at making everyone think he was just an average guy who came up with a great game. But she knew better. Alicia was okay with giving him a little bit of information, but not too much.

"So, the call?"

"Yes. The call." Memories of that morning run to the

airport, the rush to her childhood home, the disappointment and grief that she had been too late. "My father had been shot. I had to try and reach him."

"And did you?" he asked quietly.

"No. He died about two hours before I made it back."

"Well, at least he died not knowing you whored yourself out."

"Devon!" Dee said. "Don't you dare speak to her like that."

Dee walked over to the table and set two coffee mugs down. Then she gave Alicia a sympathetic look.

"I apologize for Devon. From the time he could talk, our mother said there was a nasty streak in him. He doesn't get his way and he strikes out. She always said I was the sweet one."

"Where's my coffee?" Devon asked.

"Over on the counter."

He tossed her a dirty look but rose to go get it. Dee shook her head.

"He's a handful at times."

Alicia knew Dee was being overly nice because she thought she could get some information. Still, Alicia couldn't help but relax when Dee smiled at her.

"How far along are you?" Alicia asked.

"Just four months. I think we're having twins."

"Micah isn't here to freak out so you don't have to say that," Devon said as he rejoined them.

Dee laughed. "It is fun to mess with him, considering his need for control. His face goes pale every time I say the word twins."

Alicia's smile faded when Devon sat down with the same mean frown on his face.

"So, where do we go from here?" Devon asked.

"I don't know where you're going—except away from here."

"That's unacceptable."

Anger surged. She opened her mouth to argue, but Dee stopped her.

"I think loud voices will catch Bridget's attention," she said.

Alicia nodded. "Especially for Bridget. We live a very quiet life."

"You are both angry and knocked off center by this."

Alicia ignored Devon and concentrated on Dee. "I don't trust him. You have yet to give me any proof you didn't have anything to do with my father's death."

"Guilty until proven innocent?" Devon asked, his voice dripping with sarcasm.

"In the business, that's the way it goes."

"If we don't come up with some kind of agreement, we will be here all night. And, I am pregnant. Not only do I have to constantly be fed, not to mention relieve myself, I have a very big, very protective husband who used to be a bounty hunter."

The warning in Dee's voice told her all she needed to know. Alicia had been right, but she didn't blame her. If the roles had been reversed, Alicia would have done the same thing.

"Okay, okay. I will agree not to leave."

Devon wasn't happy. He crossed his arms. "Surrender your passport."

She snorted. "Not bloody likely."

Dee took her hand. "I promise that I won't let him do anything stupid. Please...my brother had left the CIA by the time this was going on. He had to thanks to a homicidal family member—not me. I can promise you that he had nothing to do with your father's death."

With a sigh, Alicia said, "I promise I won't leave. We can meet again tomorrow."

Devon opened his mouth to argue, but Dee stepped in. "Take what you get Devon. She didn't have to agree. And let's be honest, there is a good chance she has several passports with different names."

Alicia couldn't help it, she chuckled. Dee was probably as smart as her brother.

He nodded—once.

"Good, well, we better get going. Micah has texted twice, which means he's getting antsy and you know better than to let my husband get that way."

Devon wanted to argue. She saw it in his eyes, but he relented for his sister.

"Okay. But now that I know who you are, there will be no hiding. Not anymore, so running away will be useless."

"Oh, good Lord," Dee said. "Dial down the big bad agent attitude."

She poked her brother, urging him on.

As they walked to the door, Bridget came running down the hall. She was holding a piece of paper.

"I made you a picture," Bridget said, grinning. She

handed it to Devon. "It's of our house and me and Mummy."

Devon hesitated, then took the piece of paper.

"That way you won't forget about us."

He continued to look down at the picture, then he swallowed. The silence lengthened and Bridget looked at Alicia. Confusion stamped her features. Then she turned to face Devon again.

"You don't have to take it if you don't want to," Bridget said.

"Thank you," he said, his voice hoarse with emotion. "I would never forget about you."

Bridget giggled and ran back down the hall. When he straightened, Alicia saw a flash of vulnerability in his eyes before his gaze hardened.

"Don't leave Seattle."

Then he turned and walked out the door. Dee sighed. "And they think that women are temperamental. I know you don't know me at all, but I promise you, from one mother to another, I will make sure that Devon doesn't do anything stupid. And I promise you, he would never do anything to hurt you or Bridget."

She thought back to the expression on his face when he looked at the picture. He wasn't as tough as he wanted her to think. She nodded.

"I better go catch up with him. Oh, wait." She dug into her purse. "Lord, when did I end up with so many crayons in my purse?"

Alicia smiled. "Just get used to it. It doesn't get any better."

Dee looked up at her. "I need to get a bigger purse."

She pulled out a business card, then grabbed a red crayon to circle something on it. Dee handed it to her and she blinked. It was to a BDSM club in Hawaii.

"My husband owns the club," she said with a smile. "The number is mine that I circled. Is there some way I can get a hold of you?"

She nodded and grabbed a piece of paper. "Please, don't give this out to anyone. I...I don't share a lot with other people."

"No problem. I can completely understand that. We totally need to talk about why Devon felt the need to run away that morning. We'll call tomorrow."

As she looked out the front door, Alicia realized Devon had parked his SUV behind hers in the driveway. Dee walked to the driver's side door. Alicia couldn't hear what was being said, but she was pretty sure Devon was being ordered out of the car.

Words were exchanged and Alicia watched—thoroughly amused—as the former CIA trainee and one of the most dangerous men she knew, stepped out of the SUV. He gave his sister a nasty look, but he walked around the other side. Dee looked back at Alicia and it was easy to see his sister's smile. She watched as they both got in the car and Dee backed out of the driveway.

She shut the door and turned to find Bridget standing behind her.

"They were nice. Especially Dee."

Alicia nodded. "Yes."

Bridget chewed on her bottom lip. "The man doesn't smile that much."

She thought back to that night in Las Vegas. "He used to."

They walked back into the kitchen and Bridget watched her as she cleaned up the table.

"Why did he sound funny when he talked?"

"Why did he…"

She trailed off when she realized what Bridget was talking about. "Maybe he's not used to getting such pretty pictures."

"Oh. Okay." She accepted that answer, like most four-year-olds would. Alicia knew some day it wouldn't be so easy to explain things away. Then, this life she had been living would bite her in the ass.

"How about we have some spaghetti and meatballs for dinner?" Alicia asked.

Bridget smiled. "Yummy."

"Go on and play. I'll call you when it's done."

Bridget skipped out of the kitchen and Alicia sat down at the table. She had so much to think about, and she didn't know where to start. The only thing she knew for sure was that no one would hurt her little girl.

five

In the last few days, Devon had ridden a sick rollercoaster wave of emotions. Now, he was numb. He couldn't even drum up an emotion about how he felt at the moment. He needed to regroup, recharge...think about things. Unfortunately, Dee wouldn't shut the hell up. The one emotion he could accept was irritation. Sisters just didn't know when to stop poking the bear.

"You need to stay out of it, Dee," Devon said as he walked down the hall to the apartment they rented for the vacation. She had been berating him since they left Alicia's house. Dee was the worst when she got something between her teeth. It made it very hard not to resort to their child-hood scuffles.

"You wouldn't even have a phone number to call her if it hadn't been for me."

How many times had she said that to him in the span of thirty minutes? At least five freaking times. There was only so much he could take off the woman, even if she was his twin.

Devon unlocked the door and ignored his sister. Micah was sitting on the couch in the living room.

"If either of you wakes up Alana, I might just have to beat the shit out of Devon." Dee walked over and gave him a kiss. Micah touched her stomach. "How are you doing?"

"Doing just fine, although, I'm starting to get hungry."

"You're always hungry," Devon said. He looked at Micah. "And why just me?"

"Because, Dee is the light of my life, carrying my child." He looked at Devon. "So?"

"She's definitely Dev's. She has his eyes."

"I don't need you to answer for me, Dee."

She made a face but thankfully shut up.

Micah didn't take his gaze from Devon. "And?"

Devon dropped into the chair beside the couch and scrubbed a hand over his face. He hadn't had a good night's sleep since that day at the market. The days had all started to bleed together and he knew soon he would crash. Before that though, there was always a chance for him to make some very bad decisions.

He sighed. "And nothing for the moment."

"You just left your daughter there?" Micah asked.

"Well, he doesn't have a right to her," Dee said.

That sent rage coursing through his blood. "I have every right to my daughter."

Dee shook her head. "I didn't mean like that. I meant legally at the moment. You couldn't just snap her up and leave. And besides, you wouldn't want to do that. It would scare Bridget."

He agreed, but it didn't make him any happier with the

situation. Truth was, he didn't know much about little girls. Or little kids in general. What he did know he'd picked up in the last couple of years after spending time with Alana. He definitely wasn't an expert. And, even though he was furious with Ali, she was the girl's mother. He did not believe depriving Bridget of the one person she trusted in the world. That would make him a monster.

"What's your next move?" Micah asked.

He shrugged. "I know that Alicia, or whatever she's calling herself these days, isn't going to keep me from my daughter. Or she seemed to agree to it right now."

"Why didn't she contact you before?"

"She thought Devon had something to do with her father's death. We didn't get the whole story. And let's face it, Devon isn't that easy to find."

"I was an assignment."

He spat out the words, irritated that more than his ego hurt over that. He had never forgotten her, dreamed about her most nights, and yearned to touch her again. He had been a job to her and now a man she feared. For him, it had been an experience that touched his soul. If she hadn't ended up pregnant with their daughter, he wondered if she would have even remembered him.

"Okay, I think we need to back up, because I'm confused."

"I can't explain it all. She didn't tell us the entire story. Her—our—daughter was there and I didn't want to alarm her."

"So she's in the business?"

He nodded. "I should have known."

"How were you an assignment?"

"She came looking for me because her father had been interested in me for some reason. He had been missing. That's about all we got out of her before we left."

"Show him the picture."

Devon rolled his eyes. "I'm not going to show him the picture."

As usual, Dee ignored him. She sat down on the couch next to Micah.

"It was so sweet. We were talking to Alicia and Bridget, that's the girl's name, went and drew him a picture. Then Devon took it and put it in his wallet."

Dammit. Dee fooled a lot of people with her sweet smile and big blue eyes. They always thought she was an empty headed idiot. She wasn't.

"How did you know?"

"It wasn't in the car when I got there and I knew you didn't get rid of it."

Micah looked at him, then said to Dee. "Hey, babe, why don't you go check on Alana?"

Dee looked between them and nodded. She kissed Micah on the cheek and then rose to check on their daughter.

Micah studied Devon for a long moment. "Listen, I don't like to butt in—"

"Bullshit."

Micah continued on as if Devon hadn't said anything. "But you need to make sure you get your head screwed on straight. A few years ago, I wouldn't have the first clue about this, but I do now, thanks to your sister. Once you know you have blood in this world, you don't ever let them go. We can stay for a while since Evan has been running the club with the help of Danny."

"Thanks," he said. "I thought about sending you back to Hawaii. Jay could return here and wait for me."

Micah leaned back on the couch. "Now, son, you should know better than that. Dee isn't going to let me leave you here on your own. And whether you like it or not, we're family and you're stuck with me."

He gave him a smile. "You might not believe this, but I am pretty damned happy Dee married you."

"That makes two of us."

He stood and decided to grab something to eat before heading back over to her house.

Micah didn't ask where he was going. "Get some coffee so you don't fall asleep."

Devon waved behind him as he walked out the door.

"So, he's going on a stakeout?" Dee asked as she walked in.

Micah nodded and glanced at her. "You're not mad I let him go, are you?"

She shrugged. "No. I had a feeling he would go watch over her."

"He's going to make sure she doesn't run."

Dee shook her head and sat down beside him. "No. You didn't see that house. It isn't just where they live, she's made a home. There were pictures on the walls, and it was well cared for. And, you didn't see his face when he got that picture. He looked stunned."

Micah heard a suspicious sniffle. When he looked at her, he saw the tears. She had been the same last time during her pregnancy. The truth was, he didn't know how to deal with it this time around any better than he did last time. Dee wasn't a woman who shed tears easily. So, he did the same thing he always did. He patted her knee.

"He'll be fine. He comes from tough stock." He kissed her on the nose. "I know that for a fact."

She smiled at him. "He's not as tough as I am."

"No way." He glanced back at the closed door to their room. "Is Alana still sleeping?"

She nodded, as she sniffed.

"So, we're all alone in this big, beautiful apartment without a meddling brother and a sleeping child?"

She smiled. "Yes."

He eased her back on the sofa. "Whatever will we do with our time, Mrs. Ross?"

She slipped her hands up to his shoulders. "I'm pretty sure you can come up with something."

He chuckled as he leaned down to kiss her and forget about all their troubles for at least a little while.

ALICIA TUCKED BRIDGET INTO BED, then sat beside her. She was exhausted, as if she'd been on a three day stakeout. Every muscle felt strained and every one of her bones ached.

She was only thirty-years-old and she felt as if she were three times as old.

"Do you think the man will come to visit again? You said he would."

She nodded. Since Devon and Dee had left earlier that day, Bridget could not stop talking about Devon. She was definitely intrigued by him, but Alicia had waved the concern away. It probably had more to do with the fact that he was a man. Other than service or deliverymen, there had never been any in the house.

"Do you think he'll be here tomorrow?"

Alicia thought back to the look on his face when he had accepted the picture.

"I'm pretty sure he'll come back tomorrow or the next day."

Bridget yawned, as her eyes started to close. Alicia leaned down and kissed her forehead.

"Sweet dreams, poppet."

She rose from the bed and walked toward the door, stopping just as she stepped over the threshold. As Alicia looked at her, Bridget turned over on her side, her breathing eased into a steady rhythm.

Alicia decided to make some tea and then head to bed. Just as she reached the kitchen, the lights flickered three times, signaling someone had broken through her hundred yard perimeter.

Panic came first, surging up so fast that her head spun. Bile rose in her throat as she tried to pull herself together. As soon as she had her head screwed on straight, in the next second, she ran back toward Bridget's room. Her daughter was still sleeping since the alarm hadn't hit the second stage yet.

Alicia squatted by the bed and gently shook her daughter. "Bridget, we have to go."

Her daughter sat up, her eyes barely open. "What's wrong, Mummy?"

"We've got a situation." She pulled her onto the floor and looked at her. Alicia kept her voice as even as she could even though fear danced over every nerve ending. "Now, I told you something like this could happen. We need to get out of the house and we need to do it as quietly as we can."

Bridget's eyes widened but she said nothing. She was her mother's daughter after all. Bridget nodded and slipped out of bed to the floor beside Alicia. She picked her up.

"Wrap your legs around me."

Bridget did as ordered, and Alicia stood and ran out of the room. She stopped along the way to get the 9mm she had stored inside the hallway linen closet in the safe. She had to give up a minute or two for their escape time, but she didn't want to go unarmed. The cold metal felt familiar as she wrapped her hand around the weapon.

She crouched down as she ran toward the front door. Then, she stopped, fear lancing her heart leaving her almost breathless. A large, dark figure loomed in the hall doorway.

"Ali, let's go. Someone's coming through your backyard." She knew that voice, would never be able to forget it.

Relief filled her. "Devon?"

"Yes. Come on."

He came to her and took Bridget from her arms. "Come on."

"No."

"I don't have time to fuck around. There are at least five in the back. We can argue later."

"I have a bag to take."

"Get Charles!" Bridget yelled.

"Right."

She stopped in Bridget's room, picked up her favorite bear and the go bag she had packed for Bridget. Then, she grabbed her own and was following Devon out of the front door. They ran to his SUV, which was parked in front of her driveway. He put Bridget in the backseat.

"Strap yourself in, Bridget," Devon said. He popped the trunk and Alicia threw the bags in. Then she slipped in beside him.

"Go."

He didn't argue. Instead, he hit the gas and they went raring off into the night. Alicia's heart was pounding hard against her chest and she couldn't catch her breath. She made sure the safety was on her gun before setting it down on the floorboard, then strapped herself in.

"You were right, Mummy. He did come back."

She smiled and looked at Devon, then at her daughter.

"He did, poppet. He really did."

And thank God he did. She could have gotten them out of trouble, but it was definitely easier with Devon there.

"Where are we going?"

"Back to the apartment I rented for us here."

For a moment she was confused, but then she realized he was talking about his sister and her husband.

"I don't know if I want to do that."

"You really don't have a fu—"

"Watch it," she said. He glanced at her, and she motioned with her head toward Bridget.

He sighed.

"And, what I meant was I didn't want to put your family in any more danger."

"What makes you think they'll link you and me?"

She realized that on this one point, he was correct. He continued driving, making sure to double back a few times.

"I really appreciate this," she said. "We'll find a new place soon."

He didn't say anything for a few minutes as he continued to drive. Then, he glanced up in the rearview mirror to check on Bridget. She also looked and found her daughter asleep.

"Let's get one thing straight. You and Bridget will not be out of my sight until I know that both of you are safe. There is no discussion. I will take care of both of you, but if you refuse, you go alone. You will not walk off with my daughter."

Six

The rain started to fall about five minutes from the apartment. Devon turned on the windshield wipers as he tried to come to terms with what just happened.

He had been sitting out on the street, keeping an eye on the house, and he'd seen a movement. It had taken a moment or two for him to figure out exactly what he was seeing. They'd been dressed from head to toe in black, appearing almost out of nowhere.

When he'd finally realized what he was seeing, he'd slipped out of his SUV and headed to the front door. The fact that she was already getting out of the house told him she had been prepared for it.

Of course she was prepared for it. She was the daughter of a master spy and former MI-6.

"You seethe very well in silence," she said, enough condemnation to make him grind his teeth.

He stopped at a light and looked in the mirror to check on Bridget. She was fast asleep. Fury still poured through him as he tried to calm himself down. How many times had his daughter been in danger?

He tightened his hands on the steering wheel until his knuckles were white. It was that or lose complete control. When he felt he was calm enough, he decided to start asking questions.

"How often have you had to do that?"

She didn't answer right away. He hadn't been able to hide all the anger that now boiled in his gut. He knew Ali was calculating just how much to tell him.

"You mean run?" she asked.

He nodded.

"This makes the third time. It is the first time for Bridget though. I had to run from England after my father's funeral. Then, to America after her birth, so she doesn't really remember that of course. I don't understand it at all."

"We'll figure it out when we get back to the apartment."

"I can't go there."

He ignored her as the light turned green and he pressed the gas. No way was he going to accept that. If he put her in a hotel, she could disappear forever and he would never find her. With her background, there was a very good chance she had multiple identities in who knew how many countries. She would dissolve into the population and Devon would lose his daughter.

"You will come with me to the apartment."

"Devon, I can't put Dee in danger. She's pregnant and has a baby. I would never forgive myself if she were hurt."

Again she surprised him. Of course, she was a mother now, so that might be the reason. Still, it eased some of his anger—for the moment. Thinking of his sister before her own safety was more than he expected.

"First of all, you don't know my sister that well. She can beat the crap out of a lot of people—even pregnant. Second, you haven't met my brother-in-law. He'll take care of her. Plus, I need his advice about this. Like Dee said, he's a former bounty hunter. He knows how to help people disappear."

"I don't need his help. I was fine until you showed up on my doorstep."

He turned into the parking garage and pulled into his spot. They were going to have to cut their vacation short. There was no way around it. Or he could take Ali and Bridget away and book a flight for Dee, Micah and Alana.

She checked her gun, undoing the safety, then slipped out of the car. No conversing, no questions—just cold and methodical. She kept the gun out as she surveyed the area. He stepped out of the car and did the same.

It was stupid, but he was turned on by it. There was something sexy about the lethal way she walked around the car. She nodded at him, and he popped the trunk. She headed to the backseat and leaned in to get Bridget.

"Let me take her," he said.

She didn't even turn around to respond. "I've got her."

And she did. With ease, she pulled her daughter out of the car and straightened.

"You get the bags."

She hesitated and that pissed him off. For a long moment, she studied him, but she handed Bridget over to him. He took her into his arms, and she made a few little sleepy sounds kids made. Then, she moved this way and that, trying to get comfortable. She finally settled her head on his shoulder facing his neck.

Devon pulled in a deep breath as his heart squeezed tight. It was hard to even come up with words to describe what he was feeling. And, there wasn't time to deal with it. He had to somehow get them out of Seattle alive and figure out who was actually after them.

They walked silently to the elevator, and took the entire ride up in silence. When they reached the apartment floor, he waited for Ali to step out then followed her. After unlocking the door, they stepped into the apartment.

"No security?" she asked.

"Normally, but they knew I was out and there is a little one sleeping."

She nodded.

"Why don't you set that down over there," he said, motioning with his head. "I'll take her back to my bedroom."

He started walking to his room and Ali came with him. It annoyed him but then, it made her a good mother. If the roles were reversed, he would have behaved the same way. She pulled back the sheets and he placed Bridget there. When they walked back to the kitchen, Micah and Dee were there.

"I think we need to have a little chat," Micah said.

WHEN SHE SAW Devon's pregnant sister sitting at the table, guilt swamped Alicia. Worse, there was a very stoic, huge Native American god standing behind Dee's chair. His hair was a long waterfall of black silk, and he had the most amazing red-gold skin. He watched her as if he would tear her heart out if she said one wrong thing to Dee.

"I'm sorry if we woke you," Ali said.

He nodded in acknowledgement. "No worries, as we say back home."

"Which is Hawaii."

Dee nodded. "Oh, I just realized you haven't met Micah. Micah, this is Alicia. This is my husband Micah."

He nodded in her direction.

"I'll make some coffee," Dee said. "I have decaffeinated, which is what I have to have most of the time now and that sucks."

Micah frowned as his wife moved about the kitchen. Ali got the impression that he wanted to tell Dee to sit down, but he didn't. She could tell he was a man who was accustomed to giving orders. The fact that he didn't order her to sit down gave him a few more points in her estimation.

"So, what happened?" he asked, as he sat at the table.

"I was keeping an eye on Ali's house and saw some movement in the back. I went to check it out and found out there were people coming up on her."

"Wait, you were sitting out in front of my house?" she asked.

He looked at her with that cool expression that chilled her to the bone. The Stranger.

She wanted the Devon she knew in Vegas. That man had flirted with her, teased her...captured her. He had been a charmer. This man would kill her without a second thought.

"I wasn't about to give you a chance to run."

"I said I would stay."

He crossed his arms and his frown turned uglier. "And you never contacted me about my child."

Devon thought he could stand there and judge her? No bloody way.

"You might have known about her if you hadn't left me with a note the next morning."

He opened his mouth and a deep, rich chuckle interrupted him.

They both looked at Micah. "Oh, give it up, Stryker. You're going to lose. Let's not rehash, let's move forward. You two can fight all you want once we know that we're all safe."

Devon nodded and Micah turned to her. "So, tell me, how often has this happened?"

"As I told Devon, this is only the third time. And the second time it was more for peace of mind."

His eyes flashed with admiration. "That's pretty good."

"I was trained by the best." She shrugged. "I know how to disappear."

"Apparently not that well," Devon scoffed.

She looked at him. "Really? Because until you accidentally found me—and I stress accidentally—you'd given up. And I will point out that I was fine until you went sniffing around."

"That is a good point," Micah said. "But it could be a coincidence."

"In my game, there is no such thing as coincidences," she muttered

"So, what's the plan?" Dee said, as she sat on her husband's lap. He slipped his hand over her belly, a casual gesture, but it told Ali all she needed to know about the man. She might not completely trust him, but she could probably count on him for certain things. Devon had been right. This man would definitely protect Dee.

She rubbed her temples. Being compromised meant only one thing. "I need to get a new identity."

"And then what? You keep running?" Devon asked.

"I don't have a choice. I don't even know what this is about, especially since you're not involved."

There was a beat of silence and the other three shared a glance.

"What makes you think Devon was involved?" Micah asked.

"As I said, I don't believe in coincidences. Then or now."

"You mean you thought I was behind it all."

She shrugged. "My father was obsessed with finding you —or something about you. I have no idea why. I didn't get all the information he was working on, but you were on several of the notes. None of them makes sense."

He sighed and rubbed the back of his neck. "I don't know why he was looking for me, or why my name was in his notes. I'd left the Company years earlier. Hell, I don't even have a contact. And you said he used the name Devon Stryker?"

She nodded.

"That makes no sense. I was using my birth name then."

"Well, Stryker was the name he used and you were a legend at the time." She threw her hands up in the air. "I didn't get a chance to go through all his notes before I had to get out of England."

"You flew back that morning to bury him."

"Yes, or rather reach him before he died. I disappeared the day after his funeral. I had no choice."

Devon glanced at Micah and Dee. "I think I should send you three back to Hawaii without us, and we will sort this out."

"Wait—" she said, but Micah stopped her.

"That's not going to happen, Devon. We can all go back to Hawaii. Being on my home turf makes me feel better."

They were making decisions without asking her how she felt about it. She was stunned by the night's events but she wasn't a weakling. Sir Walter Hughes' daughter didn't do what other people told her to do. She told people what to do. "That's not good."

Devon looked at her. "Why not?"

"It's a place with no escape. I don't like being stuck without an escape route, and Hawaii would box me in."

"And Seattle is safer?"

She nodded. "A flight to the east sends me to all kinds of places it's easy to disappear in. Plus, Canada is just north. I didn't pick it by chance."

Although, it had appealed to her. After spending time in South Africa, she had wanted something cold and damp. The scenery, the climate, and the location had all been perfect for her. She had built a beautiful life in that house in the woods.

"Believe me when I say we won't be trapped. Plus, we have family there who can help. Remember, it's a tourist haven. It is easier to disappear there and be one of the crowd. It might be small but there are close to a million people there. Dee knows that better than anyone."

"I did hide in plain sight for a while," Dee said. "Plus, Devon just bought some huge stupidly expensive house near Kaneohe. It has a kick ass security system."

He made a face at his sister. "I know you have no problem with the pool."

She smiled. "So, there you go. You're coming to Hawaii."

Panic made it hard for her to breathe. She didn't like anyone making choices for her. "I never said I was going."

"Let me explain things to you." Devon's voice had dipped and menace dripped from every syllable. "I am taking Bridget. I want you there too, but I am not leaving her with you."

"Just what the bloody hell do you mean by that?"

"I mean that I will file papers and get a DNA test. You are an English citizen on American soil."

She crossed her arms and smiled, although she knew there was no humor in it. "For your information, according to your government and the papers and ID I have, I am an American citizen."

"Oh, where did you get your documents from?" Dee asked. "I used this guy in LA a lot."

Alicia blinked and turned to look at Dee. "What?"

"When I was on the run, I used this great guy in LA."

"This is not a negotiation," Devon said.

"Don't you understand?" she asked. "You exposed us. I have been here for years with no problem. You show up and so do whoever is after me. They have to know you live in Hawaii."

"Only part of the time. I still spend a lot of my time in Las Vegas. The house wasn't bought in my name, so while they might know I go there, on paper, I don't own anything."

Of course, he covered that. He might not have spent a lot of time in the Company, but he was definitely perfect for the life. There was a reason recruiters had been hot to get him into the program.

She sighed. "Still, I don't like the idea."

Dee reached across the table and took her hands. "Listen. I know it seems we might have exposed you. And we might have." Devon opened his mouth, but Dee held her hand up. "Don't argue with me, Dev. We have no idea what the hell is going on, or if we tipped them in her direction."

She turned her attention back to Alicia. "But wouldn't you want Devon to figure out how and who? I promise you, he can find them if they are lurking there. We have a great group of friends who can help out in this situation. It might have been what Micah said, a coincidence."

She opened her mouth to argue, but Dee shook her head. "At least give yourself and Bridget some time to regroup. And it's Hawaii. How hard will that be? She'll get to know her cousin, and you will get to figure out where to go from there. And there's always a way off the island since Devon has his own plane."

She wanted to say no. Life would be easier without Devon in it. No complications, just her and Bridget. She glanced at him. Determination stamped his features. Well, that wasn't going to happen any time soon.

"Okay," she said. "But first sign of trouble, I am gone and so is Bridget."

SEVEN

A bout an hour later, Micah and Devon settled in the kitchen at the same table by themselves. Both Dee and Ali had gone to bed, leaving them alone to discuss the situation.

Devon was exhausted, both emotionally and physically, but he didn't think he could get to sleep. His brain working through all the connections. Devon knew he would never figure out what the hell was going on right at this moment. Still, he couldn't seem to stop thinking. He'd shut down one idea and another would pop up.

"So, you have a plan?" Micah asked, bringing him back to the present.

Devon jerked a shoulder and took a sip of his coffee. He instantly regretted it. It was cold. He needed something stronger, something more fortifying. He rose and went to grab the scotch he'd brought with him.

"Grab two glasses," Micah said.

Devon did and joined him back at the table. He poured

them both a couple of fingers of the scotch and they sat in silence.

"So, you have a woman and kid to look out after."

A statement—because his brother-in-law knew his character. There was no way in hell Devon would walk away now. Knowing Ali was in danger was enough to send him over the edge.

"Yeah," he said and tossed back the scotch. He poured more in his glass. This time, though, he sipped at it. They drank in silence. Devon knew better than to talk. Micah was going through the problem in his head.

"Do you think you could have led someone to her?" Micah asked.

"I'm not sure." And that was the one thing that had been bugging him all night. Had he put his child in danger? He had just found out about her, and the idea that he might have led the intruders to the house made him sick.

"I'm going to lean heavily in the negative category," Micah said.

He studied his brother-in-law. "Why?"

"First, they would have known you went back there tonight. If they know you, they know you're trained. Alicia seems pretty well trained."

"Yeah, her father was MI-6 so it's a family kind of thing."

He smiled. "Great. You have a woman who can kill you in your sleep."

He hated to admit it, but that was kind of a turn on. She was a woman who didn't need to be taken care of...and the element of danger made her even more attractive. He had sensed it that night, felt it course through her when he touched her. She was beautiful, but that inner strength was sexier to him. Of course, the sexy underwear was fantastic too.

"Earth to Stryker."

He blinked. "What?"

"You're sitting there staring off in the distance with a goofy smile on your face."

"I am not," he said.

"Yes, you were. Daydreaming about a woman who could snap your neck."

"She can't snap my neck. Maybe. Still, she wouldn't. She had many chances before."

Micah gave him a strange look. "At least I don't think she would hurt Dee, and that's what matters."

"Why does that matter?"

"Because I love your sister."

Devon waved that away. "No, why do you say that she wouldn't hurt Dee?"

"Oh. Well, she was concerned with putting Dee in danger. And, there was the way she was looking at her. She just wouldn't hurt her."

"Don't be *that* fooled by her demeanor. She's definitely been trained. I had no idea the night we were together."

Micah poured himself another shot of scotch. Another few minutes passed before he spoke again. "Yeah, well, what about that? You're usually so cautious about women."

He had been. Except on that particular night. There had been something about her. So lonely, and it had resonated with him. When he had touched her, it felt like kismet—as if he had found the one woman meant for him.

That was probably why he had searched for her the way he did.

"Another coincidence."

Micah chuckled. "Okay, I'll let you tell yourself that lie. Are you going to call Jay?"

He nodded, thinking of his private pilot. He'd already warned Jay they might be heading back early. They definitely were now.

"I guess we should get some sleep. I take it you're riding the couch?"

Devon glanced at the couch, and knew it was going to hurt like a bitch to sleep on it. He sighed. "Yeah."

Micah turned to head to the bedroom, Devon thought about what had happened at Ali's house.

"I think we should go back by her house, see if we can get anything."

"If they didn't destroy it."

He nodded. "If they didn't—or even if they did—there is a good chance they left some kind of evidence behind."

Micah nodded. "I'll see you in the morning."

Once Micah left, Devon went to check on Ali and Bridget. They were both sleeping. Bridget was cuddled against Ali, who had her arm wrapped about the little girl. He sighed, sipping the scotch as he tried to come to terms with the way his life had changed in the last forty-eight hours. He had never thought to be a parent, but now...he had a little girl.

It was almost too much to deal with.

He walked back into the kitchen, then went out on the balcony. He sat in one of the chairs and watched as the sun came up over Seattle, mulling over what other changes were about to hit him.

DEVON WANTED to growl when Ali crossed her arms across her chest and raised her chin. Nothing was ever going to be easy with her. Never had been either.

"I think I should go."

Of course she did, Devon thought. She'd been trying to tell him what they should do since she popped up out of bed that morning. The dark circles under her eyes told him she hadn't gotten much sleep, but he hadn't either. He didn't have the patience to deal with her stubbornness. They had enough time to run to her house, then get to the plane.

"Not a good idea."

Her frown turned darker. Devon was not going to budge. He really wanted to get the lay of the land and what kind of men were after them. With her expertise she could help, but she was still upset.

"But there are things I want to get. You might not understand."

He found the tone in her voice mildly offensive. Maybe he hadn't finished training, but he had eluded the Company for years. He studied her for a moment or two longer and then looked at Micah, who shrugged. No help from that end. Devon took Ali aside. If she wasn't going to listen to reason, he would use the one thing in this world that would get her to do anything.

Devon straightened his shoulders. "I would rather you stay here."

He thought he heard her growl. "I would rather go."

"Listen, it might be kind of hard to see your house if they blew it to smithereens. I also want Micah to get a look."

"What good is he?" she asked, then she looked at Micah. "No offense."

Micah smiled. "None taken."

"So?" she asked him.

"He was a bounty hunter. He could tell what kind of men are after you."

She snorted. "I can handle that myself, thank you very much."

"Are you okay with Bridget being left here?"

Alicia opened her mouth to argue, but stopped. She looked at Micah and Dee. Then back to Devon. "Okay, I better stay. Not that I don't trust you two, but Bridget might not like it."

And that was the crux of the thing. Anger was now riding her temper to new heights. It was more than that. Much more than that. For so long she had been in control. Sure, she was in hiding but every decision had been hers. She had been in control. Now this man she barely trusted was telling her what was best. As if some wanker who couldn't finish training knew what was best.

But what he was saying made sense. Bridget had been through so much the night before. The fact that her daughter might be shell shocked from it didn't make her any happier.

"It would probably be best if you would just make a list," Devon

She looked at Devon. He was trying to help, even if she didn't trust him completely. Hell, she didn't trust anyone, but she didn't have much choice at this point.

"But..."

She didn't want them going through her things. It was stupid because there was nothing to be ashamed of, but she wasn't accustomed to being so open with people.

"Okay. I will probably have to call the security company."

"I take it that you didn't do the regular home security people?" Devon asked.

"No. I used Dillon Security Systems. They laid it out to my specifications."

"Small world," Micah murmured.

"What?" she asked.

"We know them. Let me give Conner a call."

"I dealt with Maura. She and I got on famously."

Dee smiled. "Another coincidence."

Alicia didn't argue this time. She just let it go. She wanted to be the one to survey her house. Her training made her the best to look. Usually. This time, though, Alicia knew she was too close. And, she would feel better staying close to Bridget.

"Okay. I'll stay behind for this. But, if you have issues, call."

Devon and Micah shared a look, then they turned toward her and nodded.

"Just remember, you screw any of this up, I'll whack your bollocks off."

They said nothing as they left, shutting the door with a very definite snick.

Dee stepped up beside her. She had her hand on her softly rounded belly. "Don't worry. They won't take it personally that you threatened them."

She looked at the woman, who had the same blue eyes as Bridget. "Oh, Dee, I wasn't threatening them. If they screw anything up, I *will* whack their bullocks."

eight

Alicia had just finished cleaning up the dishes from breakfast when Dee walked in with a frown.

"Are you okay?" she asked.

Dee nodded. "I'm fine, but you didn't have to do that."

Alicia blew out a long breath. "I have to do something. I might go mental if I just sit here."

She smiled. "I understand that. Drives Micah crazy that I can't always sit and just be. I've been working since I was seventeen. I was put on bed rest with my last pregnancy. Micah was ready to tear out all of his beautiful hair. I couldn't help it. I felt so lazy. I knew I needed to be there, but still."

Alicia nodded. She completely understood that. "My father always said time spent daydreaming was wasted time."

"Well, I wouldn't go that far. A little bit of dreaming can be a good thing." Dee shook her head. "I didn't daydream for a really long time. Not while I was on the run."

"You mentioned something about that last night."

She motioned with her head to the table. Alicia followed her and sat across the table from her.

"Well, my father tried to have me killed. Devon too."

Alicia blinked. For a second, the words didn't compute, when they did, she opened her mouth once, then closed it.

Dee laughed. "Yeah, everyone has that same reaction."

Alicia sat down. "Your father tried to kill you?"

She nodded and rested her hand on her belly. "I overheard him having a man tortured, then killed. We didn't know it, but Dad was Mafia."

"You had no idea your father was in the Mob?"

"I take that back. We had an idea he was connected. I mean, a lot of our friends had fathers involved in some way." She shrugged. "Devon was always gone to some nerd camp, and I had...well, we were teenagers. What were you doing at seventeen?"

"My father had me along with him on a job in..." She paused trying to remember where they had been. "Thailand. I liked Thailand."

"Wait, your father took you on jobs when you were in high school?"

"Yes. After my mother was killed, he didn't like leaving me with anyone. I went along."

There was a look of horror on Dee's face.

"What?" Alicia asked.

"I can't imagine going on spy jobs at that age."

She shrugged. "It was good training. I learned a lot."

"You did this from the time you were twelve?"

"Part of the reason was safety. The other part was learning from my father. He knew they would pull him from the field very soon and I needed to learn from the best."

Dee studied her for a moment, then shook her head. "Anyway, I was hiding in my dad's office. I wasn't hiding to begin with, but I wasn't supposed to be there. Heard my dad, then hid in the closet." Dee shuddered. "So, I went to the FBI. Dad ended up finding me though and I went on the run for years."

Alicia worked through all the information. "That was when Devon was at the CIA camp."

Dee snorted. "I guess we can call it that. So, tell me more about your father."

Alicia sighed. "He was all I had in the world after my mum died."

"You were close?"

She thought back to their time together, then further back, before her mother had been killed, before the paranoia had set in. She remembered the three of them, a unit. They had been careful and she was sure there were measures her parents took to ensure her safety. Still, it had been a normal childhood. There were vacations and fun times at holidays, then everything had been destroyed in a matter of seconds.

"We were. My mum was killed by a terrorist bomb. Not really directed at her. Just wrong place, wrong time. Dad never really got over it."

Dee nodded.

"And then, I went into the business. I know that he watched out for me, but did not meddle. He believed that I should make it on my own."

"And you did too."

She nodded. "I was getting rather good...then it just sort of went to shit."

"But you have Bridget."

She thought about her daughter and smiled. "Yes. I have her."

Dee opened her mouth, then hesitated.

"Go on."

"I just want you to understand Devon. He was always kind of...I don't know broken."

"You're twins. He was broken but you weren't?"

"Things happen for a reason, right? Or that's the way I always looked at it. But, for us, it was so damned horrible. I had to go on the run after someone from the FBI sold me out. I didn't let anyone close for a really long time. It was too dangerous. Trusting someone could put their life in danger or mine. I just couldn't take the chance."

"And Devon? Didn't you trust him?"

"I thought he was dead. There was an accident...thanks to my father. Devon survived, but he lost his girlfriend."

That put a different light on his disappearance. Following the timeline in her head, it would have been around the time the CIA went into panic mode looking for him.

"We were so young at the time, but I know that he has always felt he was the reason she was killed. Dad thought he was in the car. So, Devon disappeared."

"Oh." Everything made a lot more sense now. When she had read his file and the case studies of his character, there was nothing that would convince her he had been selling secrets.

"So, he's probably going to be horrible with you two. Just know where he is coming from."

Alicia frowned. "What do you mean?"

Dee sighed. "He'll do anything to keep you safe. And it means he is going to be a pain in the ass. I just wanted you to understand why."

She crossed her arms beneath her breasts. "I can take care of myself and Bridget."

Dee chuckled. "Don't be getting your panties in a bunch. I know that, and to an extent he knows that. But he has a history, and just keep that in mind. I don't want you to kick his ass and make him cry like a girl."

Alicia smiled. "You think I can?"

"I'm pretty sure you can. What do you train with?"

"Some boxing."

"Me too! Well, until I got pregnant."

"You're having two so close together."

"I want to have a ton of them, but Micah wasn't happy at first. He didn't do so well during the last pregnancy. He declared we wouldn't have any more children after the incident in the delivery room."

"What incident?"

"He almost passed out. As it was, he got woozy and his stomach didn't handle the miracle of birth that well."

She thought back to the stoic Native American and joined in the laughter.

"Now *that* I might have paid to see."

MICAH AND DEVON pulled into the Ali's driveway and found that nothing had been disturbed. There was a bit of fog hanging around the bushes that lined the walk.

"It's fucking eerie, man," Micah said.

Devon nodded. There was something oddly quiet that coated the area with a thick layer of menace. It left a knot in his stomach. There was something very wrong about the house.

They both silently slipped out of the car. He watched his brother-in-law scan the area. Devon knew he was good at things like that. He'd been trained by the CIA, even if it was just preliminary training. Years of avoiding his father and brother had made him cautious. But Micah, he'd made a living at it. When he had gotten out of the business, he'd been more well-known than Dog the Bounty Hunter. Add in his rough upbringing, Micah was probably one of the most perceptive people he knew.

Micah nodded, indicating that he didn't sense anything and Devon could go in. As they walked, Micah continued looking around them. Devon approached the front door and found it locked. He used the key Ali had given him, and then walked in carefully.

It looked exactly the same. No windows were broken, nothing was damaged. In fact, he would never have guessed someone had been there that night. They walked around carefully, checking things out. It was the oddest kind of crime scene. He knew the people who had shown up last night had been sent to at least retrieve Bridget. When Micah joined him in the kitchen, he looked at Devon.

"It's like last night didn't happen," Devon said.

"Makes me think someone didn't want anyone to notice what was going on. And, maybe they think she's on her own. If so, that's good. They'll assume that she's on her own."

"That makes sense with the report that Ali got this morning. The cops went by last night, nothing looked out of place."

"Let's check out the bedrooms."

They came to Bridget's first. Again, nothing was disturbed. The covers were pulled up over the pillow, but other than that, it looked natural. They made their way down to the master bedroom.

They slipped in and it looked the same. Ali had been dressed, but her bed was in the same order. The quilt had been pulled up over the pillows. Micah looked in the bathroom and came out shaking his head.

Devon pulled the bed linens and found the pillow had a bullet hole in it.

"Fucking hell," Micah muttered.

Anger pumped through Devon as he spun around and strode down the hallway to Bridget's room again. He grabbed the sheets and yanked them down. The pillow had one small bullet hole in it. Micah stepped into the room.

"They weren't sent here to gather information or even to capture her," Devon said.

Micah walked around the bed, and Devon raised his gaze to meet his brother-in-law's.

"You're right. They were sent for one thing."

His rage grew. "Assassination."

nine

I t was amazing how fast everything came together. They had the apartment packed up, along with the things from her house, and they were heading to a private airport before three that afternoon.

Still, after witnessing how fast Dee threw their stuff together—probably learned while she was on the run from her father—Alicia worried about the danger they would face. Just being connected with her put their lives at risk. Needing to reassure herself, she approached Micah. He was the most level-headed of everyone involved and she needed his approval.

"Are you sure about this?" she asked.

"I said it was fine," Devon said, butting in. Of course he was butting in. He'd been doing that since he showed up and her life had gone to hell.

"I didn't ask you," she said without looking at him. "I was asking Micah, because my presence is a danger to his wife and children. Their safety is more important than your ego."

Devon didn't argue with her, but she could hear him cursing beneath his breath.

Micah's lips twitched once, then, he said, "I'm sure. We will add a little extra security to the house and to the club. I've already talked to Conner about it."

"Conner Dillon?"

"Yeah. I told you we used them too."

"I never talked to him. I thought he pretty much left the running of the company to his partner and his sister."

"We have a connection that goes back a long way," Micah said, looking at Dee. "And he lives in Hawaii now and handles the work in Hawaii. I think they do a lot of personal security in the Far East and Australia now as well."

"Does the entire bloody world live there now?"

Dee chuckled. "We like to lure them over. Anyway, I'm sure he'd like to talk to you about things. Give you some advice."

She snorted. "I appreciate that, but I don't need a former FBI agent's advice on security."

Dee opened her mouth but Devon stopped her. "The one thing I've learned is to avoid those interspook arguments."

"You actually learned that from your very short tenure with the CIA?" Alicia asked before she could stop herself.

"I left on my own. *I* decided to leave."

She didn't know what was making her so reckless, but she didn't care. "I'm sure most women would fall for that, but remember, I'm MI-6."

"Used to be."

"Yes, well, *I* didn't make that decision, now did I?"

He stepped so close his chest brushed her breasts. Irritation and surprisingly, arousal, sparked through her blood. "Is that the truth? I guess you call it a decision, I call it someone in your organization taking matters into his own hands."

She opened her mouth, but Dee interrupted them. "Hey."

"What?" they both said at the same time.

"You two need to cool it before the kids hear."

That brought her back to earth. She couldn't believe she'd lost her temper like that. Well, not as an adult and definitely not in front of Bridget.

"Sorry. I should have controlled myself better."

"Sorry," Devon mumbled. He picked up the last of the bags and followed Micah out the door.

Alicia shoved a hand through her hair. "How embarrassing."

Dee laughed. "No. Micah and I argue a lot. It's all that sexual chemistry."

Alicia blinked in response. The woman said the oddest things. "There is no sexual chemistry."

Dee gave her a look of pity. "Oh, honey, there is a lot of chemistry, sexual and otherwise. Tell me this. How do you feel right now?"

"Feel?"

Dee nodded.

"What do you mean?"

"Your body, how does it feel?"

"Well, kind of hot."

"Hmm."

She threw her hands in the air. "It was just an argument."

"Can you tell me that there was a point you didn't know whether you wanted to slap him or kiss him?"

That was a little too close to what she had been feeling. What the hell was going on with her? She had been losing control of everything in her life, and now she was getting hot about a man she had no business messing with—especially considering the situation.

"I plead the fifth."

With that, Alicia turned and walked off, ignoring Dee's laughter and praying she wasn't right. Getting tangled up with Devon Stryker was something she'd barely survived the first time around.

DEVON WAS STILL irritated as he stepped off the elevator. The woman was always trying to dismiss him. At one time, he might have let her do it. Now, though, his daughter was involved.

That was a lie. Even if Bridget had never been born, the moment Devon saw Ali again, he would have hunted her down.

"You might as well just let it go," Micah said. He'd been talking in that calm "I know better than you" tone since they'd left the parking garage. If he didn't shut the hell up, there was a good chance he would punch him. Then, there was a good chance Devon would get his ass kicked—a very big chance.

"I heard you the first five times you said it."

Devon knew he sounded like an ass. He didn't really give a damn. The argument with Ali had left him on edge and out of sorts. It hadn't even been that much of an argument. But one little disagreement and he'd been on the verge of yelling at her—or taking her to bed.

He opened the door and strode across the room. He said nothing to his sister as he went through the room making sure they'd gotten all their belongings.

His sister watched him from her seat in the kitchen and just like him, didn't say a word.

"What's the matter?" Dee said.

Micah kissed her cheek. "Nothing a little one on one time with Alicia wouldn't fix."

He snarled at Micah and Dee laughed.

"Where are Bridget and Ali?"

"I think it's odd you call her by that name," Dee said.

"Who cares?"

This made Dee laugh even more.

"They're in your room, getting ready. Bridget has some jitters about the plane."

He said nothing as he turned and headed in that direction. He'd had about three hours of sleep, if that, and he was...out of sorts. That was it. Just out of sorts.

And really freaking horny.

Fuck. He leaned against the wall and counted back from ten. Then, he did it again. This wasn't the time or place. They had too much shit on their plate to deal with. Not to mention, they had an innocent little girl in danger.

That brought him back to earth. There was a little girl,

and she needed both of them to protect her. As if on cue, he heard the two of them talking.

"I've never been on a plane before," Bridget said, nerves leaving her voice tight with worry.

"You have but you were a little baby then, so you don't remember."

"Still. And this is a *little* plane."

"We'll be fine, poppet. These are nice people and guess what?"

"What?"

"I heard they have all kinds of little gadgets, including a shower and a bed. Isn't that exciting?"

"I suppose." The girl was definitely not impressed with that.

Devon moved closer so he could see in the room. Bridget was sitting on the bed and Ali dropped down to squat in front of her.

"Right now, we can't go back to the house. I told you it might happen."

"But I like our house. And the woods. You said maybe next year we could get a dog."

"I know and it might still happen. We just have to deal with this problem, then maybe we can make it back."

She sighed. "Hawaii doesn't sound like much fun."

It was easy to hear the pout in Bridget's voice. It took every bit of his control not to interrupt and tell her he would take her anywhere she wanted to go.

"I have a feeling a lot of people would disagree with you."

"Yeah?" she asked as she sniffled.

"Yeah. There are beaches we can go to each day. And, I heard a rumor that Devon has a pool."

"It's too cold for swimming."

Ali shook her head and smiled. "Not in Hawaii. You can do that year round."

"Really?"

"Yes. And Dee said there's whales there right now. We might get to see some."

Her hatred for Hawaii apparently forgotten, Bridget clapped. "I love whales."

"I know you do. Now, what did I tell you about us doing things?"

"We can do it if we do it together," Bridget said.

"That's right," Ali said. "Now give your mum a hug, and we need to get going."

She nodded and did just that. He watched, as he swallowed a lump in his throat. He had missed so much of his daughter's life and he still blamed Ali for that, but the people behind the attack and her father's death were the most to blame for it.

When he got a hold of the bastards, he would make sure to make them pay.

THE FORMER AGENT looked out the window, watching the rain as it slipped down the glass. This time of year was known for being rainy and cold. It set the perfect mood.

"And you say that they were nowhere to be found? Did you stake out the house?"

The younger man shifted his feet. "They weren't there."

"Are you telling me you just left?"

"It was compromised. She was gone."

The agent sighed. All these years and good help was still hard to find. People had no real work ethic anymore. "You've fucked this one up."

"I—"

"No. Go back to your post, Williams."

He hesitated. The agent knew he wanted to argue, but he finally left.

"You want him fired?"

The agent looked at the second in command. "Fired. Yes."

"Do you want Smythe to take care of it?"

Smythe handled their terminations. It wasn't something they used that often, but this definitely warranted swift and devastating action. They hadn't been this close to Alicia Hughes in years, and he had fucked it up good. Lying in wait, because Alicia would have returned at some point, should have been the next course of action. Instead, the wanker had fled the States, running back to London with his tail between his legs. And he should pay for that.

Decision made, the agent nodded. Left alone, the agent sat down in front of the window and plotted.

ten

W ithin three hours, they were on their way across the Pacific. Devon knew Ali and Bridget were overwhelmed, but they handled it like troopers. Knowing they needed to discuss their next move, the girls had been settled in the bedroom of the plane. The cousins were fast friends and good at entertaining themselves.

The girls seemed to be dealing with all of this better than he was. In fact, Devon was barely keeping it together. The images of those pillows with the bullet holes kept playing through his mind. He still had to break the news to Ali. He knew she wasn't going to handle it well, and there was a chance she'd try to run. Putting him or his family in danger was very upsetting to her.

"My house is secure enough, but when I talked to Conner, he said he'd come by and discuss it tomorrow," Devon said. He looked at Ali. "He was very impressed with you."

"Of course he was. I've never spoken to him personally, but I pointed out some holes in his security measures. Maura seemed pretty happy to tell him about them too." She snorted. "FBI, they spend more time shopping for ray bans and suits."

He couldn't stop his lips from twitching. Her voice was filled with arrogance and, dammit, he found it attractive. He always hated women who played the victim. Ali was definitely a woman who would always stand and fight. It made her almost irresistible. Her outward confidence had attracted him as much as that tight, athletic body of hers. He remembered the taste of her flesh, the way she moaned his name...

"Earth to Devon." Micah said.

Devon blinked, coming back down to earth. When Devon turned to look at his brother-in-law, he found Micah smiling at him.

"What?"

"Nothing. Maybe we need to bring the girls out here, and you can go take a nap."

He rubbed his hand over the back of his neck trying to ignore the pulse of lust that now beat through his blood. He was still pissed at Ali, but the attraction was as strong as ever. Worse, he kept seeing her steal glances at him, and he was starting to realize the mutual attraction was still there.

He was insane to be so damned hot for a woman who could kill him.

"I think the house is fine, but I told him I wanted a review of the security we have on it." He looked at Ali. The images of the night before came flashing back to him. "I just realized that you were on your way out of the house the other night. How did you know?"

"I have silent alarms set to go off if someone breaches my land within 100 yards."

He looked at her. "That's kind of fanatical."

She shrugged. "If it was just me, I could handle the typical alarm, but Bridget brings other concerns. The silent alarm allowed me to get her out of there without frightening her too much."

Of course, Ali had thought of that. Being raised by someone in MI-6, there was a good chance she could run her own security company. Considering the measures she took just to protect her house, Devon was amazed that she'd been found out.

"I'll talk to Evan and let him handle most of the Rough 'n Ready issues right now," Micah said. "Hopefully, we won't have to do this for very long."

"Evan?" she asked. She looked at Devon. "I don't want any more people involved."

"He's my business partner and he's family," Micah said. "It's going to be impossible to avoid telling him. Our lives, personal and business, are intertwined. He'll be good at deflecting questions about my absence at work. It will be noticed."

"If it's noticed that my brother-in-law is missing or taking a long absence after what happened in Seattle, that will get noticed. You and I both know that."

She opened her mouth but Dee stopped her. "I know you've handled this by yourself for so many years, that it's hard for you to accept help, but believe me, Evan is trustworthy. And, we won't tell him anything more than is necessary, for our safety and for his. Evan and his wife are expecting their first child."

She studied Dee for a second then nodded.

"Do you think it will be suspicious that you aren't around the club?" Devon asked.

Micah shook his head. "I was supposed to be off until the end of next week anyway. By then we should have a better handle on this. We can always blame it on Dee."

"Thanks a lot," she said with a laugh. Then she sighed. The tired sound reminded Devon that she was pregnant, and she hadn't had a good night's sleep.

"Why don't you go take a nap?" he asked her.

"The girls are back there."

"Well, go recline somewhere. I don't think any of us want to relive the horror of your previous bed rest."

She frowned at him then looked at Ali. "See what I have to put up with?"

Ali laughed and the sound danced through his blood. It was so rare to hear that he felt like a junkie waiting for the next hit.

"Yes, well, be happy with it, and I suggest you take advantage of it too."

Dee yawned. "I guess I will. Especially since I have a sexy man to rub my feet."

"I love you, but I will not rub your feet," Devon said.

Dee smacked him on the arm. Micah just chuckled and helped his wife out of her seat. They moved further back in the plane leaving him and Ali alone.

"There's something you're not telling me," she said.

Devon hated that she was so perceptive. It made it hard to keep things he would rather she not know from her.

"I told you everything."

She gave him a look that told him she knew he was lying, but she let it go.

"When we get there, Evan will be picking us up. I usually hire a driver because the flight is such a bitch, and with Dee and Micah, plus the kid, it's just easier. But in this situation, I didn't want to take the chance. We filed a flight plan, but other than that, we didn't raise any red flags. Also, we are going to go with the idea that Dee needs some more rest or has an appointment. I think Evan will spread the word at the club. It is a microcosm and Oahu is like one big town. Annoying sometimes, but it will work for this. I still highly doubt they've made the connection, but I would rather be safe than sorry."

She nodded. "And after we land?"

"What do you mean?"

"Where will we be staying? Do you have a hotel or maybe a rental that you could suggest?"

"I have a five bedroom house, so that will be where we stay."

When she didn't instantly agree, he narrowed his eyes. "You will be staying with me. It has high security, and it's better to be on your own home turf if we're attacked. Plus, I have an out in the back."

"What do you mean?"

"My house backs up to Kaneohe Bay. While it leaves us a little exposed, it also gives us another way to get Bridget out of there."

She sighed. "I just feel odd."

"What do you mean?"

"I mean, depending on someone else, and just going along with what you say."

Blunt. And it was one of the things he liked about her.

"I thought this was the agreement. Why are you freaking out over staying somewhere safe until we get a handle on this?"

"I just told you. I've been making decisions for both of us since she was born."

"Well, whose fault is that?" he asked, irritated with her again. Why couldn't she just give in every now and then?

"I don't know. Maybe it was the wanker who left me a note the next day."

He opened his mouth to argue, but she shook her head.

"I can't do this right now. I'm tired and angry about the situation. We are never going to resolve *that* argument. We both know it."

"Okay. But we will be having a discussion about this later when everything gets settled."

She hesitated, then nodded.

"Get some rest," he said.

"I was going to check on Bridget."

"I'll do it. You're going to need your strength because I have a feeling that little girl is going to need you more than she needs me after we land."

She didn't say anything for a moment, then a small smile curved her lips. "You're right. Thanks."

An emotion he couldn't define moved through him. She looked so damned thankful for that one small gesture. All of a sudden, he felt awkward. She was smiling at him, and he didn't know what to say.

He rose out of his seat and grabbed a blanket.

"Lay back."

For once she did as he told her, and he laid the throw on top of her. He had to fight the urge to rub the backs of his knuckles over her cheek. It was an intimacy he didn't have a right to, but he wanted it. Yeah, he was still pissed about Bridget and missing out, but there had never been another woman who hit him in the gut like Ali did.

He just had to protect her and Bridget...then they could figure out where they went from there.

ALICIA STEPPED off the plane and immediately noted the differences. She had spent the majority of her life hopping from one place to the next, never really staying anywhere for very long. She never had issues acclimating to a new climate or culture. Now though, things were different. She'd grown accustomed to her dark Washington woods and the cool weather.

Here, the air hung heavy with humidity and the scent of exotic flowers. Even on the tarmac, she could smell their fragrance. She pulled out her sunglasses and slid them on. It wasn't too bright, but the sun still brightened the sky amongst the few stray clouds that lingered in the area. Again, she had become so accustomed to gray skies and cooler air.

A tall, rangy man with a wealth of golden brown hair

came walking across the runway towards them. He was dressed casually, as she assumed most people in Hawaii did. The mirrored sunglasses hid his eyes, but the smile he offered was as warm as the Hawaiian sunshine. He was by himself. Four leis were draped over his forearm.

"Well, you must be Devon's," he said, slipping a lei over her head and kissing both her cheeks.

"Excuse me?"

Instead of explaining himself, his smile widened. "I'm Evan Chambers.

The South colored his voice. She heard a hint of South Carolina and maybe Georgia there, but another aspect caught her attention. It had to be the influence from Hawaii. She had heard it in Micah and Dee's voices. He pulled off his sunglasses.

"I'm Alicia Hughes and this is my daughter Bridget."

His smile widened and she had to blink. A set of dimples appeared and the man's eyes fairly twinkled. She was embarrassed to admit she felt downright flustered. In fact, she found it hard to come up with what to say to him.

He apparently was accustomed to it. He winked at her and looked down at Bridget. "Hello, princess."

Her daughter glanced up at the tall man and said nothing for a second. Bridget apparently was stunned by the charm tossed in her direction. Then...she giggled.

Alicia shook her head in amazement.

"Don't worry, all the girls giggle around Evan," Dee said, walking up beside Alicia.

"Except for you," Evan said, leaning forward to put a lei on Dee, and then he gave her a fast, loud kiss on the lips.

"Oh, please. You couldn't deal with a woman who could kick your...butt."

He chuckled. "And there is the other princess."

Alana came running to him and he picked her up. She gave him a large smacking kiss—much like the same one he had shared with Dee. This was a family, she thought. They weren't all related, but she could see the connections easily. Evan might not be blood, but he was like an uncle.

"How was Seattle?" he asked.

"'K and I have a new friend," Alana said with a smile.

Evan put the last lei on her. "I heard. Now I have another princess to spoil."

"Yes." Alana clapped. "And we can swim in Dev's pool."

"You always know what's important," Evan said.

Devon and Micah brought up the rear, duffle bags in their hands.

"Hey, Bra," Micah said. "How are things going at the club?"

"Pretty good. Although, I've told Danny if he wants to take over running the club and give up being a doctor, we would be happy to hire him." Evan looked at Devon. "I heard you had some issues."

"Just a few," Devon said with little emotion.

"Someone chased us out of our house," Bridget said.

He looked at her then he squatted down to her level. "That wasn't very nice. But, you have a new friend and you're in Hawaii, so that's good. And, like Princess Alana said, you can go to the pool."

She smiled at him. "Yes."

He looked up at Alicia and winked again, then he straightened. "Are y'all ready to go?"

"Got a couple more bags," Devon said.

"Let's get off this tarmac," Micah said. "Devon and I will load up the bags."

Evan turned and headed to the SUV.

"How's May?" Dee asked as they followed him.

"Fat."

"I'm telling her you said that. She's pregnant with your child, you should be nicer."

"Too late. I'm in trouble for calling her feet fat. I was showing her concern and told her to call in to work today and take off. You would have thought I ran over her favorite dog or something. Then, she called her father who is now threatening to disown me. So, not sure you telling her that is going to hurt me anymore than that. Her father said something about disowning me because she called to cry to him."

Dee laughed. "I don't blame her. May is Evan's wife and my best friend."

When they got to the massive vehicle, there were two child seats in the back seat. He easily got Alana settled and turned for Bridget.

"Oh, I can take care of that," she said.

He shook his head. "No worries."

He had both girls settled easily, then he sat between them.

"I can sit there, Evan. You don't look that comfortable."

He smiled at her. "See, you don't know me or you would know that as long as I'm surrounded by women, I'm happy."

She opened her mouth to argue, but Dee shook her head as she took the seat on the driver's side.

"Let it go. He is really telling the truth."

Inwardly she shrugged and took the other seat in the second row.

Micah and Devon were there within a few moments, and they were on their way out of the airport. She sat back and watched the lush Hawaiian landscape fly by. She would feel better once they were settled at Devon's house. She knew there was a lot to be done...and even more they would have to work out. But getting to the bottom of all of this was more important. After that, maybe she and Devon could come to some understanding.

With a sigh, she shook her head. Her brain was just too jumbled to think straight. She would worry about other things once she knew her daughter was safe.

eleven

Devon and Evan went up to the house first. They surveyed the surrounding area, then Devon unlocked the front door and disarmed the alarm. They walked through house, making sure nothing had been disturbed. When they were both satisfied with the house, Devon started back to the front door.

Evan stopped him.

"Do you need anyone around to help?"

Devon shook his head. "Ali has training, and with this system, we'll be fine. Besides, May is too far along for you to leave her for too long."

"Yeah, but there's always my brother-in-law Danny."

He thought of the younger man who had a reputation at Rough 'n Ready for liking older women.

"I appreciate it, but we don't need the help."

Devon resumed making his way to the front door, ignoring the nagging voice in his head. It wouldn't hurt having the man there to help out, but he just couldn't do it.

He didn't want another man around Ali at the moment. It was stupid, but every time they encountered a man—even ones like Evan and Micah—he had to deal with his need to beat the hell out of them.

He didn't know how to deal with the jealousy. It was new and annoying. Since his time in high school, he'd never really been a man who got jealous. Women were important to him; he respected them and enjoyed them. He never understood the emotion. It seemed like a waste of energy, but at the moment, thinking of the young fire dancer hanging around Ali made him want to tear off the man's arms and beat him over the head with them.

"Okay, but let me know if you change your mind." Evan tossed Devon a knowing look. "And for your peace of mind, I'll let you know he doesn't poach."

Devon stepped out the front door and snorted to cover his embarrassment. Evan was a little too close for comfort.

The older man said nothing as he walked to the SUV, but Devon got a glimpse of the knowing smile curving his lips. Evan and Micah could get on a man's nerves. Now that they were both happily married and producing offspring, they always thought they knew best. It was more than a little aggravating. Evan went around to the back to get the bags as Ali stepped out and helped Bridget down. They walked quietly up to the house.

Evan sat the bags down. "I better be getting home. I have some making up to do with May before she heads to Dupree's and makes Chris cry." He turned to Ali and Bridget. "E Komo mai."

"Thank you."

He nodded toward Devon and walked back to the SUV.

They watched him drive away and Ali said, "You don't lack for characters in your life, that's for sure."

He followed them into the house, shutting the door and setting the alarm. Bridget said something and Ali leaned down so she could whisper in her ear. Ali nodded and turned to Devon.

"Where's your bathroom?"

"Down the hall on the left."

She nodded and walked down the hall with Bridget. When she returned, he noted the dark smudges beneath her eyes. He was sure he didn't look much better, but he hated seeing her like that. It was a stupid thought, one that spoke of a connection they didn't have. It didn't quell the over-whelming need to give her comfort.

"Is she okay?" he asked.

Ali nodded. "She's fine. A little overwhelmed, but I think that has more to do with the fact that she just had her first plane ride—that she can remember at least—and the fact that we are in Hawaii."

She turned around, looking at his living area. It hit him; he had no idea on what to do next. The only women he had in his house had been his sister and her best friend May. He hadn't felt the need to bring a woman back to the house because he hadn't had a date in months. For some reason, in his own mind, he had been waiting for this woman. It was insane, but for some reason, it was one idea that he kept coming back to.

He was still pissed, but some of that had faded. Now, the need he had always had for her rushed through him. One night, almost five years earlier, and he still wanted her. In fact, he knew without a doubt that even without the situation—including Bridget—he would have done just the same.

"You're making me nervous," Ali said, breaking into his thoughts.

He glanced at her. She had one arm across her chest, her hand clutched her other arm. It was an awkward look for a woman who always looked so self-possessed. He knew she rarely showed any kind of vulnerability to anyone.

"Sorry. Just, now that I have you here, I don't know what to do with you."

For a long moment, she didn't say anything. Then, slowly, her lips curved into a seductive smile. "You didn't have a problem with that before."

All the air between them seemed to thicken and the breath evaporated in his lungs. The sultriness of her tone shot straight to his gut. It was as if all the years they had been apart dissolved. Heat surged, his stomach tightened, and his cock twitched. Just like that, he wanted to strip her down and fuck her until they were too tired to talk.

Her face flushed and her gaze darted away. "I apologize. I don't know why I said that."

Again, he was surprised by her. Seeing her so unsure of herself touched something in him. It was there that night in Vegas and it was there now. She presented herself as an independent woman who had a backbone of steel. But just like when they first met, he sensed a vulnerability beneath that hard-edged surface. It made him want her even more.

He wanted nothing more than to be her soft place to fall, but he knew they had issues. Mainly someone was trying to kill her and their daughter. But, when they were through with it all, he would be there. He wasn't quite sure what he wanted but he knew he wanted Bridget in his life...and something more with Ali.

He smiled and stepped closer. He lifted his hand— hoping that she didn't see the way it shook—and brushed her hair back from her face. "No, don't be sorry."

Even he heard the way his voice deepened over the words. Standing this close her, Devon caught her unique scent. He breathed it in and his head spun. His heart hammered against his chest as he leaned closer. Just a taste, it was all he needed.

"Devon," she said, but he barely heard his name. It filtered over his flesh and sunk down into his soul. Something teased his senses. After a long moment, he realized it was her. What scared the hell out of him was the thought that it would always be her. Just her.

He was less than an inch away, so close he could feel her sweet breath on his lips. The moment before he could close the space between them, Bridget came bouncing back into the room.

"Mummy," she said running toward them.

The two of them sprang apart as if they had been committing a crime.

Devon stepped back, drew in a deep breath and had to get his body back under control. Jesus, his blood was still humming with need. He shoved both his hands through his hair.

"Did you wash your hands?" Ali asked.

Bridget held her hands up as she nodded.

When Devon felt as if he wouldn't embarrass himself, he turned to face them.

"I think Bridget would like a bath, wouldn't you, poppet?"

Bridget smiled up at her mother, then at him and nodded.

"Of course. There are a couple of rooms up here with a Jack and Jill bathroom that I thought would work."

He grabbed their suitcase and Ali grabbed another bag that had their toiletries. They follow him up the stairs.

"Did you build this house?" Ali asked.

"No. It had been on the market for a few months when I found it. I wasn't really looking at buying a house here, but after Dee had Alana, I wanted to be close by. We're the only blood family that each of us trusts."

"But you didn't want to stay with them?"

"I did a few times, but I like my privacy."

"I can understand that."

"Yeah?"

"I was an only child who spent a huge part of her childhood in foreign countries. With my training, large crowds irritate me."

"You can never be too sure with lots of people around," Bridget said in a tone most kids would use to repeat grammar rules.

Ali said nothing as they walked down the corridor to the room. He decided to fill the gap.

"Being in a house with Dee...there is no privacy. She's been like that since we were kids. She'd just barge into my room without knocking. Still does."

When he reached the first room, he turned and found her smiling at him.

"What?"

She shrugged. "I think it's nice you have someone like that. I would have killed for a sibling when I was growing up. My parents were surprised by me, so there were no others."

He heard the wistfulness in her voice. He wanted to comfort her, but he didn't have that right. Bridget ran into the room.

"It looks like a princess room!"

He nodded and smiled. "The house came with all the furnishings."

Ali smiled. "And you kept it because Alana would like it."

Admiration filled her tone, and he suddenly felt his cheeks heat up. He was fucking blushing. Good lord.

Before he could embarrass himself further, his phone went off. He knew the number.

"I have to take this. Let me know if you need anything."

She nodded and he walked out of the room.

Then he answered. "Stryker here."

"I hear we have a situation," Conner said.

"More than one, but this one seems to be controlled at the moment."

"Maura's been working on the threat assessment. She wanted to come over here because she felt she failed Alicia."

Conner's main office was in Miami, where his sister and his partner ran the main part of the business.

"There really is no need for that. In fact, that system is why Alicia and Bridget are still alive."

"That's good to hear, but we also helped Alicia with

monitoring her security in the virtual world. We had no idea she had been spotted by someone."

He thought back to that day he saw her and the way he found her.

"I wonder if they used security footage to zero in on her?"

There was a pause. "You know, with the right kind of programs and enough help, whoever is after her could have done that. That will make it impossible to figure out who did this."

"How long have you known who she was?" Devon asked.

"From the beginning. She knew if we started to dig for her, that we would find the layered identity. Only Maura, Rory, and Zeke, plus me, know about her true identity. The three of them worked on her case exclusively, and we didn't let anyone else know about it."

That was interesting. Conner was always a little overzealous when it came to security. The fact he was so strict about Ali's case told Devon he knew how serious the situation was.

"I think we're fine right now, but how about a meeting in the morning? We can go over some of the assessments," Devon said.

He heard some tapping against keys as he waited for Conner's answer. "There's one person I want to bring with me. Sean Kaheaku has been doing some consulting for us, and I think he would be very good to help."

"Are you sure you can trust him?"

"Yeah. He can be an ass, but he's one of the best in the

security business. He's related to Eli St. John in a round about way."

St. John owned and operated a cattle ranch on the Big Island. His previous career had been in the Australian Army.

"I would rather he didn't know too much before he got here."

"No problem. Truth is, I would love to have him working for me full time, but he doesn't like to settle."

"Okay, how about nine tomorrow? I would start earlier, but we're all pretty tired."

"No problem. See you then."

Conner hung up without saying goodbye. Devon smiled. Conner had always been a little different. FBI to his core, he had a long connection with Dee and for that Devon had put up with him. But, he also found the man to be a solid security expert.

He thought they needed some more food and decided to see if the girls needed anything. Devon stopped. Girls. It was a term that Micah had used on more than one occasion when talking about Dee and Alana. That proprietary air...his girls.

Dammit, now he wanted that. He wanted the right to call them *his* girls. He had known about Bridget less than four days, but he already felt a connection to her—and Ali... well, she still made his knees go weak.

He shook those thoughts away. He would deal with that as soon as they solved their main problem. Wanting to head out and get the food so they could get Bridget to bed, Devon hurried up the stairs.

"THIS HOUSE IS REALLY BIG," Bridget said as she followed Alicia into the bathroom.

Alicia didn't correct her daughter's assumption. It was probably a mansion for Hawaii where land was scarce and expensive. For a girl who grew up on an estate in England, it wasn't that big. Of course, it was bigger than the house they had in Seattle. She just hoped they could return soon.

Alicia shook those thoughts away and walked to the French doors. Opening them, she drew in a deep breath.

It was breathtaking.

Leave it to Devon to get a house with a view like this. They were in a bay, which gave the house a sense of tranquility she assumed was hard to find on Oahu. There was an old wooden dock where a canoe was tied up. The pool was big and oval, included a waterfall, and some kind of turtles painted on the bottom. There was a hot tub.

"I want to go swimming."

She chuckled as she smoothed her hand over her daughter's golden hair. "First, I don't have a bathing suit for you. You need a new one. And it's late. Bath first tonight, then we'll have a snack and you can go to bed."

"Okay."

The disappointment was easier to take than the fear that was quickly returning. She knew that someone had breached the levels of security she had spent years constructing. It wasn't someone who just happened upon the information.

"Hey," Devon said from the doorway.

"Hey, Devon. Mummy said I can't go swimming tonight."

Devon looked from her daughter to Alicia. "Why not?"

She rolled her eyes. "Because, she doesn't have a bathing suit that fits. We can get one tomorrow."

He shrugged and looked pitiful. "Sorry, kid. Gotta listen to your mom. Is there anything you need from the grocery store?"

"Could you make sure to have some oatmeal? It's Bridget's favorite for breakfast."

"Your wish is my command. Do you want anything, poppet?" he asked.

Hearing her pet name for her daughter should have made her angry. It was private, the name only *she* used for Bridget. Instead, it sounded right, even in his horrible American accent.

Her daughter opened her mouth, but Alicia knew Bridget well.

"He's not going to get you a suit."

Devon chuckled. "Trust me, you don't want me picking out your clothes. Ask Dee. I'll be back in a few minutes."

She nodded. He stepped closer, as if to lean in to kiss her. It would be a normal thing for a husband and wife to do. Then, he pulled back, apparently just realizing what he was doing. He shook his head and headed down the stairs.

It was just like that moment earlier. She knew if Bridget had not interrupted them, he would have kissed her. Alicia had seen it in his eyes, the need he had for her...and the intent.

And she had wanted him to do it. Wanted to be touched.

Alicia closed her eyes and drew in a deep breath. She looked down at her daughter.

"We better get you cleaned up before he gets back."

Bridget nodded and ran into the bathroom. Daydreaming about Devon wasn't going to help her solve her problems.

She had proven that once before, and the lesson had been one of the hardest in her life.

twelve

Devon returned in less than an hour. He was happy that Ali hadn't fought him that much this time about staying behind. He knew she hadn't even thought of going with him. She wouldn't put Bridget in danger and, right now, that was her primary concern. It wouldn't last of course. She just wasn't a woman who could be tied down.

Worse, he had to keep putting off the long talk he felt both of them knew they needed to have. It lingered in the back of his mind, a constant irritation that he couldn't discuss with her yet. Too much was going on right now, and the safety of their daughter was just as important to him. The other factor was Bridget. Alarming her with a discussion of her parentage wouldn't be smart. It also wouldn't give him any traction with Ali. Still, Devon needed answers. Lots of them. After the rush to get back to Hawaii, things were settling down. Their protection was important, but his mind was capable of seeing past the danger now. It was time for explanations.

Bridget and Ali joined him as he cooked the hotdogs he'd bought. It wasn't the most nutritious meal, but he didn't know what to buy. He had walked into the grocery store and almost had a panic attack. He didn't know what girls her age ate. Worse, he worried he would pick something she hated and he would be judged by a four-year-old. Because, a bad ass computer expert was tied in knots over a little girl.

Pathetic.

"Hey, Devon," Bridget said, as she walked over to the table.

She was dressed in a Frozen nightgown and her hair had been brushed back from her face. She was so damned cute and precious. Devon had to resist the urge to brush his hand over the top of her head. Instead, he grabbed Hawaiian macaroni salad and some cut up fruit.

"I hope you like hot dogs," he said.

"I do. Mummy doesn't let me have them often."

He glanced up at Ali. "Considering the circumstances, I think we can indulge for one night.

As they sat down, he saw Ali survey the area. In truth, he was pretty sure she didn't even realize she was doing it. It was part of her training, probably from an early age—considering what her father did for a living. It was as second nature to her as breathing was for a normal person.

He stifled a sigh. He hated seeing her that way. There was a fine edge to her nerves and he knew she was stressed. She never let on to Bridget, though. As they sat and ate, she joked with her daughter and talked of plans for Hawaii.

Every now and then, he could pick up on her tension. A glance at her daughter, a sharp look when she heard a strange noise...she didn't miss anything. Neither did Devon.

"I think it's time to head to bed, poppet," she said.

Bridget frowned. "I'm not tired."

Then she defeated her own argument by yawning.

"Let's go, Bridget. We'll have lots of fun tomorrow swimming. You need your rest though. What do you say to Devon for dinner?"

Bridget gave him a sweet, sleepy smile and his heart turned over. How this little slip of a girl could undo him so easily was beyond him. Right now, though, he wanted to beat the shit out of the bastards who had scared her that night in Seattle.

"Thank you, Devon. It was yummy."

Ali smiled in approval, then she stood and picked her up. "I'll clean up as soon as I get her in bed."

He couldn't talk yet. There was another freaking lump in his throat. He watched Ali take her upstairs and felt something loosen in his chest. Too many emotions were rushing through him, and he needed time to work through them. He had learned at a young age to keep himself busy while he thought out things that were bothering him.

With that in mind, he decided to clean up the dishes.

ALICIA GOT Bridget into bed with a minimum of fuss. Bridget barely argued about it, even though she had a pretty long nap on the plane. Alicia sat on the edge of the bed and watched as Bridget's eyes closed. She brushed a lock of hair off her face.

It seemed so odd that they were in Devon's house in Hawaii. Less than a week ago, he had been more than a passing thought. No, that was wrong. Every time she looked at her daughter, she saw Devon. Those eyes were unmistakable. If ever a time she thought she could forget about the man who fathered her daughter, Alicia just had to look at her.

When she was sure Bridget was sleeping, Alicia made her way down the stairs to talk to Devon. He wanted answers and she couldn't blame him. But...she still didn't trust him completely. He was keeping things from her. Something went on at her house that he wasn't telling her. Micah and Devon considered themselves good liars, but she could always spot them. It was one of the reasons she'd been trained for interrogation. And those two had not been telling her the truth. They had told her shades of the truth, but important things were missing.

She made her way back downstairs to Devon. It would take her a long time to get used to the house. Everywhere she looked there was wood. It was open, airy, and seemed to be part of the environment. It was hard to tell where the house ended and the outside began. He was sitting at the kitchen breakfast bar. The dishes had been stowed away, the counters were pristine.

"I said I would clean up."

He shrugged as his gaze followed her every move. The anger had dissolved, but she knew he didn't trust her. She understood that. Trust was harder to earn than anything else.

"I've been cleaning up my own messes for a while."

She didn't miss the double meaning.

He sipped at a golden-brown liquid she assumed was whiskey. He said nothing, but kept watching her. Something tickled at the back of her throat as she waited for him to say something...anything. And, truth was, she was usually good at this. With all her training, she didn't normally have an issue with a stare down, but this one was starting to get on her nerves. It made her uncomfortable in so many different ways, she didn't know which way to move.

"Stop that."

Cool amusement danced in his eyes. "What?"

"We were both trained, and I know all the tricks. You want answers, ask. Otherwise, stop trying to play games with me, Devon. I promise, you will lose."

"Is that the truth?"

"Yes. Remember, I was raised by a master spy. I know all the games. I know the strategies to win and I rarely worry about who gets hurt in the outcome—unless it's Bridget."

He set his drink down on the counter and sighed. The sound was oddly lonely. She didn't think a man like him lived a very lonely life. He was a millionaire, if not a billionaire. Those type of people always seemed to be surrounded by others.

But now that she thought about their time together, he didn't seem to have anyone in his life. No handlers or hangers' on. He didn't have entourage. Unless she counted sister, brother-in-law, and niece.

"You said you couldn't find me?"

Right to the point. This she could handle. She nodded.

"But, you found me once. I assume MI-6 sent you."

"Yes, I found you, but that was all me. I worked outside of the borders of MI-6. I called in a few favors, but there was nothing official. They didn't know your connection to my father, and I was on vacation when I went looking for you."

He frowned. "Why?"

Those frantic days came rushing back to her with such blinding force it left her a little dizzy. She rarely thought of them now, but whenever she did, Alicia's stomach pitched. Desperation had been her companion as she wondered if she was looking for a dead man. She had been trained for every situation in a spy's life, but that. Searching for her father had been out of the realm of her knowledge.

"My father was missing. I'd been looking for three months before I found you."

"I still don't understand the connection." Confusion stamped his features as his brow furrowed. "For the life of me, I really can't remember his name. Well, the name is familiar, but I know nothing else. At that point, I'd moved on from the CIA and wanted nothing to do with them."

"I went through some of his notes. I could read his shorthand, while others couldn't. He was trying to find you. He was almost desperate with it."

And he had never come to her. To this day, she wondered why he hadn't. He was the one person she trusted in the world but after this, she had wondered if he hadn't trusted her. That hurt almost more than losing him.

"I told you I didn't know your father."

"I believe you, now. Then, I didn't know you at all. All I knew was that he was looking for you. I have no indication on why he was. It was right before he disappeared. I connected the dots."

"Doesn't MI-6 keep track of their spies?"

"Father was retired. Well, semi-retired. I know they consulted him from time to time, but he wasn't out in the field."

Devon frowned. "That young?"

She found a smile then. "My parents had given up on children when I came along. They were both spies, and after a few years of trying, they gave up. Then, when Mum was thirty-eight and my father was forty-five, I surprised them."

"You loved them."

She blinked. "Yes. They were stodgy and set in their ways, but they loved me. I didn't have a traditional upbringing, but I never doubted their love."

He said nothing as he sipped at his whiskey again. "So, your father was looking for me."

"Yes. Father had been reviewing old cases and some old scenarios. We'd had a couple of embarrassing scandals right about that time, and the higher ups were worried something else would come back to haunt us. That's all I knew about his work at the time."

"He didn't confide in you?"

"No. I don't think he could. It would be a conflict of interest, and with me still being active, that made it difficult. Father would bend some of the rules, but when it came to me, he would not compromise."

She could tell by his expression that he thought her father

should have told her. Ali couldn't argue with that because she had often thought the same thing. There was always a chance if he had told her what was going on, he might still be alive today.

"Did you ever find anything on his computer?"

"Father didn't trust computers, but he had put a password that even my computer genius cousin couldn't crack."

"So, I was off to Hawaii and you were...what happened then?"

"My cousin called. My father had been shot. He was home then, although I found that surprising because he hadn't answered the phone when I rung him up."

"And he died."

She nodded. It had been one of the worst trips of her life, frantically trying to get back to England and failing. The grief had left her stunned, numb to everything around her.

"I still don't understand why you didn't come looking for me."

"Because, he was looking for you before *he* disappeared. That's all I knew then. How did I know that you didn't have something to do with whoever ended up coming after him? After spending a night with you, I get a phone call he's been shot. You're nowhere to be found. What would you think?"

He sighed. "That we'd set you up. I'm seeing that now. But, after you found out about Bridget..." Then he shook his head. "No, wait. When did you go on the run?"

"The day after I buried my father."

It was his turn to blink. "That fast? Why?"

"My father had an Aston Martin."

Devon chuckled. "Your father drove a 007 car?"

She smiled. "It was one of his most prized possessions. I think he loved the irony of it, you know? He was known as one of the best spies England ever produced but he was far from what most people think of a spy."

"So, not a James Bond type?"

She shook her head. "Far from it. I said my parents were stodgy and they were. Father always reminded most people of someone who served in Parliament. A bit fussy, very gray around the edges. I guess that was why he was such a good spy. No one paid attention to the old guy who wore suits from the 1980s."

"You left quickly from England?" Devon asked.

"Oh, yes. I was supposed to take the car into London for a debriefing, but the weather turned bad and I wanted to take my Land Rover. The grounds' keeper, Edward, was going to drive it into the garage. It exploded."

"Just like that."

"No. It made this funny clicking sound and I knew the moment I heard it" She fought off the shiver that inevitably raced through her blood. "You don't work in the business and not know. I was running towards it when it went off. I knew then that if I stuck around, I was a dead woman."

"It's all starting to make sense now."

She said nothing else as she could almost hear his brain ticking away with all the information she had told him. One of the things she had read in the reports about Devon was he was a thinker. Not that he couldn't act quickly, but he was a problem solver. And right now, she knew she could catch him off guard because his mind was occupied with something else.

"There's something you're not telling me about my house."

His gaze finally focused back on him. "I should have known you would pick up on that."

"Of course. I knew you and Micah both were lying."

"I didn't lie."

Oh, the arrogance of men. They always seemed to think they could leave things out and she would just ignore it. First her father and now Devon. She needed information, even if it was bad. Had the story she just told him not make a dent in that big, stupid male ego?

"You just didn't tell me." She settled her hands on her hips. "That's a lie of omission."

He tapped his fingers against the glass. She knew he was coming up with some other diversion to get her off the topic. Her stomach clenched. If he was really worried about telling her, it must have been something really, really bad.

"There wasn't much damage."

She fought off a growl. "You said that."

"The only thing we found was a bullet hole in your pillow." She was just getting that assimilated in her head when he continued. "And, there was one in Bridget's pillow."

For a moment, she said nothing. Her heart had almost stuttered to a stop as she tried to come to terms with what he just told her.

"You know what this means, don't you?" he asked.

She looked up at him. "They know about my daughter."

"Yeah, *our* daughter has a big red target on her back."

thirteen

Devon was up before dawn. It wasn't something he did that often.

Strike that. He was sometimes up before dawn, but mainly because he hadn't gone to bed.

Once a hacker, always a hacker.

He smiled as he sipped his coffee and walked out to the lanai. Soft waves lapped at the small dock at the end of his property. There was a sweetness to Hawaiian air all day, but it seemed most pungent in the morning. He would have never picked Hawaii for himself, but since his only family was here, and there was no way his sister would ever leave Micah, Devon has settled there. It had started out as an occasional visit, but he had been spending more and more time over the last year. He still missed his seasons.

He set his cup on the table and settled back in the chair. As he watched the sun peek up over the horizon, Devon decided he needed to rethink his views on early morning rituals. This was not a bad way to start the day.

He'd hoped to get some sleep, but he had failed. Exhausted, he had fallen asleep quickly only to awake less than two hours later. His brain was still drenched with the memories of their night together. Hell, he could still taste her essence and hear her moans. He'd been left shivering with need and immediately reached for her. He'd found his bed empty, of course.

His cock hardened as a fine sweat broke out on his forehead. Fuck. He closed his eyes and tried to calm himself down. As soon as he did, images of having her in his bed washed over him. Damn. The woman was in his life again for less than a week and he couldn't control himself.

"How ridiculous is it that this is your view every morning?" Ali said from behind him.

Dammit, he couldn't get a break. The woman was in his head dancing through his dreams and taunting him with memories. Now he had to deal with her in the flesh.

Devon summoned what was left of his control and turned toward the sound of her voice.

The moment he did, he instantly regretted it. She was wearing a simple blue shirt and a pair of jean shorts. Her feet were bare. He thanked the Lord she was looking out at the bay and not at him. Drawing in a deep breath, he turned back around.

"Very, but I don't live here all the time. I bought this to be near Dee. We spent enough time apart."

"And because you're an uncle now," she said, taking the seat next to his. He noticed she had a cup of coffee also. "Family is really important. I get that."

She was letting him know she equated her duplicity to his need to be near Dee. In a way, he could understand it. When he'd thought Dee was in danger, he'd kidnapped her. He would do it again in a heartbeat. Family *was* important.

"How's Bridget?"

She smiled. "Still sleeping. I think it was a bit overwhelming for her."

"The granddaughter and daughter of a master spy is overwhelmed?"

He felt her glance. "I'm hardly a master spy."

"I could have been talking about myself."

She laughed and there it was again. That happy sound moved through him. It did more to tangle up his libido than any words could. He knew that most of the time, she saved her happiness for Bridget. Their little girl was too happy not to have spent time with a mother who showed joy. The sound of her laughter was like a drug.

"Not bloody likely. Let's remember, you didn't finish training."

Why did she need to keep bringing that up? "And you did."

She looked out at the bay, avoiding eye contact. He didn't know if she was uncomfortable with the questioning or him. Or both.

"I lived it. From the time I was twelve."

"Not from birth."

Her smile dimmed. "No. Before my mother...died...we lived a normal life. Well, normal for a two-spy household. After that, my father became focused on keeping me safe."

Before he could ask her more, the sound of small feet came smacking against the wood stopped him. It was one he knew from the times Alana had spent the night with him.

"Mummy," Bridget yelled, a laugh bubbling out of her throat. "There you are."

As she ran toward them, her hair flew behind her. Innocent abandonment. Not matter how irritated he was with Ali not telling him about Bridget, he knew she had done an excellent job on raising their daughter. Even after everything they had been through in the last couple of days, Bridget looked fearless.

She launched herself at Ali, who caught her without blinking an eye. He'd watched Dee learn the ins and outs of parenthood and knew it was an acquired skill. Especially without a full cup of coffee.

"Of course, I'm right here." She set the girl on her feet then smiled. "Did you have good dreams?"

"Yes. Lots." She looked at Devon. "Good morning."

He nodded and tried to think of something to say. It was all still too new to him. In the end, he did nothing more than smile.

"Did you use the potty?" Ali asked.

"Yes."

"Hungry?"

"Yes!" Then she turned and ran into the house. Devon looked at Ali, who shook her head.

"Is she always like this in the morning?" Devon asked.

"Yes. Even when she was a baby. She was always an early riser. And a happy one. It was very hard to deal with."

He chuckled as he stood and followed Ali into the house in search of their daughter.

Their daughter.

He still didn't know what to say about that. Or feel. She'd kept his daughter from him, but there had been extenuating circumstances.

"Do you think Mr. Stryker has waffles?"

"I'm not sure, because I asked him to get us oatmeal."

Bridget frowned. "I really want waffles."

Ali laughed again. "Okay, but I am not sure he has them, so you have to ask him. Nicely."

Bridget looked around her mother and smiled at him. Two little dimples winked at him. She was such a delightful mixture of both their features. Her joyous spirit reminded him of Dee. And she was his.

The air backed up in his lungs as his head spun.

"Devon," Ali said, turning to face him. She was frowning. "Are you okay?"

He nodded, but the room started to revolve. She walked over to him and touched his arm.

"I'm sorry. I don't need waffles," Bridget said; rushing forward, worry darkening her blue eyes.

He shook his head. "You can have waffles. I keep some frozen ones for when Alana spends the night. They're in the bottom drawer of the refrigerator."

Bridget smiled.

He looked at Ali, who had an understanding expression on her face. "Are you sure you're okay?"

Devon nodded. Then sat at the breakfast bar. Ali looked at him for a moment longer, but Bridget demanded attention and she turned to help her daughter. They giggled and chatted. Devon sat there, with the morning sun streaming into the kitchen, and enjoyed the view of his child and her mother interacting.

ALICIA WATCHED Devon as he and Bridget sat together eating breakfast. She knew he had been stunned by something before, but she didn't have the heart to grill him. The bare emotion she had witnessed told her all she needed to know. Devon wasn't a threat, never had been. And she had kept his daughter from him.

"Mummy, is there something wrong?" Bridget asked.

Devon turned to look at her. Dammit. The love of her life was just too perceptive for a four-year-old. Considering her parents, it wasn't something that should have surprised her, but it didn't make it any easier to deal with.

"I'm fine, poppet. I think I have some jet lag."

"What's that?"

"When you travel, sometimes you don't feel that well for a few days."

"Oh." She went back to eating her breakfast.

"Are you sure?" Devon asked.

She nodded and went to pour herself another cup of coffee.

"So, what do you do for a job?" Bridget asked.

"I invent games."

"Do you mean like Chutes and Ladders and Candyland?"

"In a way. But I do them on the computer."

"I like the computer, but Mummy only lets me stay on it for a little bit. She says it will rot my brain."

The last part was interjected with Bridget's impression of her mother's accent. Oh, bloody hell. Her face heated.

"Is that a fact?" he asked.

"Yes. She says observ...what do you call it, Mummy?"

She turned and faced the two of them. Devon was smiling.

"Yes, what do you call it, Mummy?"

Bridget giggled. "She's not your mummy."

"He's just being silly, Bridget."

"You still haven't answered the question," Devon said.

"Observation."

"That's right," Bridget said around a mouth full of waffles. "Mummy says that is more important to develop than sitting at a computer playing stupid games."

Devon looked like he was trying his best not to laugh. "Oh, is that a fact?"

"Yes."

He looked at Alicia, that sexy smile curving his lips, and she blinked. Her body felt as if it were on fire. All of the sudden, images of that smile as he looked down on her while they'd been in bed came rushing back to her. Her face turned even hotter.

"I have to agree with your mother, kid. Observing is definitely better than the imagination sometimes."

Dammit. He was making her hot and bothered just by

looking at her. His gaze swept over her body, and she could swear it felt as if he touched her. And in front of her daughter.

She crossed her arms over her breasts mainly because she was afraid he would see her hardened nipples. "I was thinking we could pick up a swimsuit today for Bridget."

Some of his humor faded. "Sorry, but we have a meeting with Conner this morning. You know, I could probably call Dee and she could pick you something up."

Alicia wanted to argue with him, but she knew it was probably for the best. It was hard for her to accept, but she was going to be forced to rely on other people. She nodded.

"If we are going to have a meeting, I better make myself presentable. Are you done, poppet?"

"I can keep an eye on her."

She hesitated, not because she didn't trust him, but because she wasn't quite sure he knew what he was getting into.

"Are you sure?"

He nodded. "I've handled Alana and she's a handful, so I am pretty sure I can handle Bridget."

"Okay. Tell you what," she said to Bridget. "Why don't we go upstairs and you can get dressed? Then you can meet Devon back down here."

"Okay." She turned to look at Devon. "I'll be right back."

He stood and helped her down. As they walked away, Alicia knew he watched them. She could feel his gaze boring into her back. But, for the first time in a long time, she felt comforted by the attention. It had been a long time since she'd had someone watch her back.

DEVON GRABBED his fishing pole as he and Bridget walked out onto the lanai. Before moving to Hawaii, he had never really fished. Being the geek he was, he didn't spend a lot of time outdoors. He'd found the pole at the house one day and spent time on the dock. He hadn't caught a thing, but it had given him time to think out a problem with a new program he was working on.

"Are there a lot of fish in the water?" Bridget asked.

"Not sure. I don't catch much."

"Oh," she said, sounding disappointed. "I hope Dee comes soon with my new bathing suit. I really like to swim."

He nodded as they walked side by side down the dock. He helped her sit down, then took the spot next to her.

"Dee said she would be here soon, and I think there is a good chance Alana is coming with her."

"Yay. I don't get to spend much time with other girls."

He would love to read Ali the riot act about that, but considering the situation, he understood her reasoning. She had been doing everything right to keep their daughter safe. He probably would have done something similar.

"So, what do you do to fish?"

He smiled down at her, then turned his attention to the pole. He set it in the water.

"This is it."

Bridget said nothing for a few minutes. He had a few nibbles, but nothing really came up and took hold.

He looked at Bridget, who was scanning the area. She looked so much like her mother at that moment it was a bit uncanny.

"What are you doing?"

"Looking. I might not get to stay here long and I want to remember it all."

That seemed a little mature for her age, but there was a good chance she had a near genius IQ. Plus, living with someone who was hyper conscious of her surroundings probably caused Bridget to be a little more observant.

"I'll tell you what."

"What?"

"You can come back here anytime you want. You and your mommy."

The moment the words were out of his mouth, he realized how true they were. He did want a relationship, especially with his daughter. Her mother...he wasn't sure of that yet.

"Really?" she asked.

"Sure, I have more than enough—oof."

She threw her arms around his neck and hugged him.

"I would love that more than anything."

"So, you like Hawaii now?"

She leaned back. "Yes, and Alana and you."

He blinked and realized his eyes were burning. She was smiling, at him, that big grin and right then and just like that, his heart tumbled out of his chest and fell with a splat against the dock. He brushed his hand over golden hair, realizing he had just fallen in love with his little girl.

ALICIA WATCHED the scene out at the dock. She was too far away to hear what they were saying, but she knew it had been important. Each moment longer they spent with Devon, the more attached he was getting to their daughter. She waited for the panic to set in. Since birth, she had kept Bridget a secret from everyone in her life, even her cousin Millie. She thought it would be best not to let anyone know there was the most precious piece of her running around in the world. If they had killed her father, they wouldn't hesitate killing Bridget.

She forced herself away from the window and tried to get her thoughts in order for the meeting. It wouldn't do to look like an idiot in front of Devon and Conner.

She pulled off her shorts and shirt, then grabbed the one sundress she had with her. After slipping it on, she looked at herself in the full-length mirror. She looked like hell. She might have had a decent amount of sleep the night before, but no amount of rest could erase the fine lines of worry on her forehead. This life on the run was aging her more every day.

She ran a hand through her hair and tried to calm raw nerves. Being in peril was her main issue, which was a definite. Seeing Devon again...that was just making it even worse. The conflicting emotions she had during breakfast and just now made it hard to concentrate. She wanted this done with so she could decide what to do about the man who had always tangled her up.

She had to get her head screwed on straight. If she didn't keep her wits about her, there was a good chance that she would miss something. From the start of all her troubles, she had known there was something off about the whole situation. Her father always confided in her. Always. They never hid anything from each other, but for some reason, he had done that with this case. She knew he trusted her, so there had to be an aspect he didn't want her to know.

What was his involvement?

Before she could work through her thoughts, there was a soft knock at the door. Then it opened and Bridget's head popped through the crack.

"Mummy, Dev says it's time for the meeting."

"Dev is it now?"

Bridget smiled and walked across the room. "That's what everyone else calls him, and he said I could call him that. It's okay, right?"

"If he said so, then it is. You're going to have to stay here while I have this meeting, but there are a lot of toys in your room. Will you be okay up here?"

Bridget smiled. "Yes."

Without a thought, her daughter turned and ran to the other room. Alicia was chuckling when she turned to look at herself one more time in the mirror. She ran her hands down the front of her dress then realized she was stalling. The sooner she talked to them, the sooner this might be resolved.

As she walked down the stairs, she heard the low murmur of male voices. Then, there was a female voice she recognized. She stepped off the last stair, and made her way to the living area that opened to the back lanai.

The first person she saw was Dee. Devon's sister turned and smiled. "Hey, there, Ali. I got a couple suits that might work for Bridget and I thought I would come over to help with Bridget. Plus, Alana here was wanting to play today and I thought they would wear themselves out."

Bridget laughed. "Spoken like a true mother. She's upstairs. I'll go get her."

"I know where. You stay here." Alicia gave her a grateful smile as she watched Dee try to keep up with her daughter.

"Alicia Hughes as I live and breathe."

She turned toward the sound of the voice and laughed. A vision from her past stepped forward. He was dressed in a custom made suit, no tie—of course, and he had the same smirk she remembered from ten years earlier.

"Sean?"

He came to her as he always did and gave her a huge hug, picking her off the ground. By the time he set her on her feet, Devon was standing beside the two of them.

"I take it you two know each other."

Sean smiled but didn't take his gaze from hers. "Yes. Alicia here and I worked a few jobs together. And when did you get rid of the blonde?"

"Oh pooh. You worked with my father. I was just along to observe."

One elegant eyebrow rose. "I think you did a little more than that." He looked up at her hair. "When did you go brunette?"

"Three or four years ago."

Sean studied her. "I like it."

"My life is now complete that I got your approval," she said, unable to keep the sarcasm out of her tone.

Sean smiled.

"And is there a reason you seem to need to keep your hands on her waist?"

She finally looked at Devon and frowned at him. She opened her mouth, but Sean just chuckled. "No worries, Stryker."

"I didn't know you'd moved back here. I heard you were working privately."

"Now that you two have had time to catch up, I assume I'm here for a reason."

She turned and realized Conner Dillon was there. "Sorry. It's so nice to meet you, Mr. Dillon."

"Please call me Conner, and the honor is all mine."

"Yeah, Conner here has a security crush on you," Sean said, slinging one arm over her shoulder.

"What?"

"Your designs. His heart went all aflutter over them."

"Oh, well, most of that my father taught me."

Conner didn't exactly smile, but she had the impression that he was amused. "What I want to know is just how they found you in Seattle and broke through all those wonderful designs to keep you safe?"

"I would like to know that, but I had been there over two years. Maybe I stayed too long."

He shook his head. "Is there anything you changed in the last few weeks, something that would draw attention to you?"

"No. Same routine, nothing different except..."

She trailed off and glanced at Devon.

His face looked like it was made of stone, then his jaw flexed. He was grinding his teeth. "Me. I'm the only factor that changed in your life in the last few weeks. Shit, I probably led them right to you."

fourteen

As they gathered around the table, Devon fumed silently, but not only because that big, stupid spy wouldn't take his fucking hands off Ali. Most of it was directed at himself. He couldn't believe he was acting like such an ass about this. Kaheaku was an old friend of her family. What's more, he'd come to help. And now, dammit, he still wanted to beat the living shit out of Kaheaku. Instead of doing that, he concentrated on what was happening around the table.

Even dressed in a pair of shorts and a Hawaiian shirt, Conner still looked like an FBI agent. Short cropped hair, the perfect posture, not to mention the lean hungry gaze, made him appear to still be working for the FBI. He pulled out his computer and started to discuss what little he'd been able to find out.

"I don't have your computer skills, but I pulled in Maura to work on it."

There was something in his voice that Devon picked up on. "Pulled her in?"

Conner's lips twitched. "Well, she pointed out that she's smarter than I am. Several times in fact."

Ali chuckled. "I think that's why Maura and I get along so well."

"You're both smarter than Conner?" Kaheaku said.

Ali shook her head. "No, we don't give a bloody damn about men's egos."

"Anyway," Conner said, "I can't seem to find any connection between you and Walter Hughes. I went through everything you gave me, and Maura played outside the lines. Nothing. There is nothing that either of you worked on, officially."

"But I do know that my father was looking for him." She looked at Kaheaku. "You know how he would get."

Sean nodded. "Walter could become obsessed over something. And it didn't always have to be about work. Remember when Facebook started? Walter spent weeks on there."

"On Facebook?" Devon asked.

Ali nodded and a smile curved her lips. "Only in the interest of research. He found it fascinating that so many people would reveal even the most personal things online. Anyone could see it. Where they lived, what they were doing...it was actually a little disturbing to him."

"Yeah, I remember that," Kaheaku said. "I think he was the first person in the industry to write up a memo about it. Breaches in security were bad enough, but with the invention of social media, so many people never gave posting what looked like useless information online a second thought. It has been a nightmare."

"But to get back to the discussion," Ali said. "Father was looking for Devon, but I still don't know why. He was obsessed with it like he always would get, but this was different. Almost unorganized and desperate."

"What do you mean?" Devon asked.

"My father was a man who organized everything. It was almost pathological. He organized his underwear drawer by color and style. So, when I arrived at the house after the funeral and found his office a mess, I was shocked. Notes everywhere and Devon's name was all over the place."

"Well, that's where it gets sticky," Conner said. "I have a couple of questions."

"Okay."

"First, with his advanced age, do you think he might have had a slip mentally?"

Devon expected Ali to get mad, but she surprised him. She pursed her lips, a sure sign she was thinking about it.

"No. There was something weighing on him, something that might have affected me too."

"Why do you say that?" Conner asked.

"With me still being fully active with MI-6 at the time, he wouldn't want to compromise me. But there is something more."

"The other option is the one that I really hate to broach, but we have to look at it just in case," Conner said.

Ali frowned. "What do you mean?"

"Your father was reviewing old cases. Maybe he either stumbled upon information that he could have, let's say, used against someone. There is also a chance that he realized something he did as an agent was about to be revealed."

For a moment, he knew she didn't understand. Then, comprehension moved over her features. Her eyes narrowed.

"My father was a lot of things. He was a bit OCD, and he wasn't always the best father and husband. But there is one thing he was not—and that was a traitor."

Conner sighed and looked genuinely apologetic. "We don't always know what our family will do in certain situations."

"I am not saying that my father didn't cut a few corners, especially when they investigated my mother's death, but he would never betray his country."

"I never said that. But the cases he was researching were all the ones he oversaw. In fact, he went back fifteen years."

She sat back. "If he was looking back that means he wasn't looking for something on himself. Why would he have to? Sean can tell you. My father had a mind like a steel trap. He could remember everything he saw."

Kaheaku stirred. "I have to agree with Alicia here. Hughes wasn't slipping, even in his old age. If anything, he was probably getting sharper. I do know that one thing he liked to do was go over old cases that went wrong."

She gave Kaheaku a grateful smile. Devon tried his best not to get pissed at the man for knowing her, but it was damned hard. He might not have anything to do with the lifestyle at Rough 'n Ready, but he handled a lot of the computer issues and he knew the clientele. Kaheaku had a reputation there as being a very sought after Dom. He had his pick of women *and* men.

"Yes, my father believed that we would always learn from our mistakes. I do know someone had given him files, so whatever he was doing was somewhat official."

"And maybe he was looking for one of his own. Perhaps Devon stumbled across it."

She glanced at him and he shrugged. "I doubt it. The only thing I check on is my name—to make sure they aren't still looking for me."

"When you were with the CIA, what did you do?" Kaheaku asked.

He still didn't like the bastard. In fact, he really hated him. Every time he and Ali shared a secret glance, he wanted to bash the bastard's face in.

"I was in a trainee program."

"I remember hearing about that. It was scrapped not too long after you disappeared. I think they thought that car wreck was a result of your computer hacking."

"Eli says you're pretty good."

"I'm one of the best. But, I don't think I found anything when I was there. I can start to do some snooping."

"That would be good," Conner said. Then he turned to Ali. "I know what you and Sean say, but I want you to be prepared that your father might have done something that caused his death."

"You want me to accept that my father was a traitor and then tried to cover it up? That is never going to happen."

Conner opened his mouth but she stopped him. "Conner, I respect you, but you didn't know my father, did you?"

"No. I knew the name but that was it."

"He stood for honor. He believed in what he was doing,

but he didn't do anything outside the bounds of his duty to the crown. He might have ticked off those above him in the chain, but he did not compromise. Nothing you can say will ever make me think that the man I knew was a traitor. Excuse me."

She shoved away from the table and walked out the door to the lanai.

Kaheaku shook his head. "Without any kind of proof, she'll never believe you."

"Was he a man who would do something for money?"

"No. The truth is, they were loaded, and probably still are. There's a reason she could hide so well. Hughes' father held patents on some kind of gadget they used during World War II, and I know Ali's mom came from an old money background. He's the one who taught me where to keep my money so I would be safe from anyone tracking me. Alicia probably has access to it."

"But if he were a traitor, the crown could freeze his assets," Conner said.

Kaheaku smiled. "If they could find them, but I am pretty sure they won't be able to even now. So, money wouldn't be the object. Truth is, the only reason Hughes would turn traitor was to protect what he saw as his most valuable asset."

"And that would be?" Conner asked.

"Alicia. He adored her. Without a doubt, her father would kill anyone if he thought they were a danger to her."

ALI STOOD on the dock and listened as the waves lapped gently against the wooden planks. Her anger had finally faded, but she was still irritated. She had spoken the truth. There was nothing in this world that would ever convince her that her father had sold out. Even if they had a picture of him handing off a classified file, she knew it would be doctored. Her father cut a lot of corners, but one thing he would never do was turn his back on his country.

She heard a creak of wood behind her and knew who was there.

"You were never good at stealth mode," Alicia said.

Sean stepped up beside her. "I wasn't trying."

She smiled and looked at her father's protégé. "Sure. So what have you been up to?"

"I'm doing some private security work here and there. Especially with Lassiter."

The name sent a little shock of alarm racing along her flesh. She didn't like the man, never had. He was former CIA and always thought the interrogation techniques they used on accused terrorists didn't go far enough.

Also, her father had hated the man. That was enough for her. Her father's instincts were *never* wrong.

"Sean, Lassiter's dirty.

He shrugged. "Not on the jobs I work."

She sighed. "You always did know how to get into trouble. Are you working alone?"

He shook his head. "No. Got some friends I work with from time to time."

"Don't tell me you and Randy Young are working together?"

"You were always jealous of him."

"First, there would have to be a reason for me to be jealous of him and there is not. I'm not any more attracted to you than you are to me." She snorted. "And with my current troubles, do you really think I need another bloody American in my life?"

Sean smiled.

"Randy. Ugh. Was that his name or a reference to his inability to control his libido?"

"His name. And I work with him from time to time along with Jaime Alexander."

She looked at him. "You're working with two of your old lovers? Sean, that's just wrong."

"You were always too much of a prude. We're just working together." He looked out over the water. "Besides, the two of them are together now."

She sensed something else in his expression. "Oh, Sean, why do you do that to yourself? You always let people hurt you."

He shoved his hands in his pockets and sighed. "Let's not go over old news, Alicia."

"I just wish you would settle down and be happy."

"I don't think you have any room to judge me, Alicia."

She shrugged. "I've been a bit busy."

He said nothing for a long moment. "So, you and Stryker?"

"He was the job. I was looking for my father and Devon was the only clue I found."

She sensed his glance.

"Is that a fact?"

"Yes."

"And, how did he get away?"

Because she'd fallen asleep in his arms and didn't want to end the fantasy. And leave it to Sean to pick up on that. "He ran off before I could question him."

"Alicia Hughes, you're lying." Amusement filled his voice.

"What's that supposed to mean?"

"You used a honey trap on him. Then, you just let him get away?"

"Yes."

He gave her a look that said he didn't believe her. "How did you hook back up?"

"He saw us."

"Us?"

Dammit. She had lost her edge over the last few years. "Us. Me and Bridget."

"Bridget."

She finally turned to face him. "Okay. See, I used the honey trap, and we used protection and I was on the pill, but I ended up pregnant. Father died right after that night and I was on the run. I was pretty far along before I realized what was happening."

"Wait, slow down. You're a mother? You can't be a mother."

That caused her to stop trying to explain. "What's that supposed to mean?"

"Because...well, just because. You are too young to have a baby."

"I turned thirty this year."

Horror moved over his features. "I don't care. In my mind, you're still a virgin."

She rolled her eyes. "Well, I was on the run. I couldn't trust anyone in England, so I went to South Africa to that estate my mother's family owns."

He shook his head. "Oh, Ali, why didn't you come looking for me? You didn't have to do it alone."

"But I did, Sean. I couldn't risk it. I was afraid I would lead whoever killed father to you. I knew it had something to do with his investigation, and I was worried you would be in danger."

"So, you leave yourself exposed? Alicia."

She heard the reprimand in his voice, but it didn't anger her. She had to speak the truth.

"I couldn't have you get hurt."

Before he could respond, the sound of little feet reached her and she found her daughter rushing toward her. "Mummy!"

And much like she had that morning, Bridget launched herself at Alicia. "Poppet, what are you doing down here?"

"Miss Dee said she could take us out for lunch and then she said I had to ask you."

Bridget looked at Sean and smiled.

"Lord." It was the only word that escaped as he looked at her and Bridget.

"Sean," Dee said. He finally broke away and looked at Dee.

"Hey there lovely lady. When are you going to leave that boring husband of yours?"

She gave him a kiss on the cheek. "Don't let Micah hear that. Last time you said something like that, he threatened to kick you out of Rough 'n Ready."

She was smiling at him and then he looked at Bridget. "That is freaking uncanny."

Suddenly what Dee said hit her full force. "Wait. You mean Sean is a member of your BDSM club?"

Dee nodded and opened her mouth.

"No. Don't. I don't want to know. It would be like knowing what my brother was doing in his sex life. Too much information."

Dee laughed. "Okay. I wanted to know what you thought about having..." she leaned forward and put her hands over Bridget's ears. "I thought maybe we could have Bridget stay over."

Alarm moved through her. "I'm not sure that would be a good idea."

"I just thought it would give you and Dev a couple days to get the security up to grade. We have a good system but then, they probably wouldn't make that connection."

"Actually, it's a good idea," Sean said.

Alicia crossed her arms. "I don't like it.

"Of course you don't," Dee said. "I wouldn't either, but if Bridget's okay with it, we can try it. If she gets upset, we can always run her back over."

"And, they won't connect you with her right now. This

way, Micah and Dee can keep an eye on her. Neighbors will just know there is a friend visiting."

She thought it over. From the day she was born, Bridget had never been away from her overnight. She looked at her daughter.

"Would you feel okay if you stayed overnight with Alana?"

Bridget clapped. "I would love it."

"You have to listen to Dee and Micah. And if you get scared, make sure you have Dee call me."

"I promise." She gave her a kiss, turned and ran toward the house.

"I can get you a few things together for her."

Dee shook her head. "I got that, if you don't mind."

"Okay."

"Alana is going to have a blast. I'll call and let you know how it's going."

She followed Bridget back up the dock and to the house. Alicia and Sean watched her go.

"You know your father didn't do anything treasonous," he said.

She nodded. "I know. But now I wonder just what the hell he *was* into. And just how it all ended up getting him killed."

"Hawaii?" the former agent asked. "What the bloody hell are they doing there?"

"I'm not sure and we aren't sure exactly where they are at the moment."

"What the bloody fucking hell does that mean?"

"Once they arrived, they disappeared. Devon Stryker has little to no presence on the islands, but his sister does. We could use her as bait."

The former agent snorted. "That's brilliant." Sarcasm dripped from every word. "No, we keep this low key. We can find her and Stryker soon enough."

The helper nodded.

"Get the arrangements made, but use one of our lesser known aliases."

He nodded. "You and I?"

"Yes. I have an idea on how to draw her out, and it will take more than one of us to make it work."

He nodded and left the room as the former agent sat back to plan the trip. Finally, this would end and life would be returned to the plans made so many years earlier.

Alicia Hughes just had to die...and then everything would be right again.

fifteen

About an hour later, they were done. Ali had returned for a few minutes while they discussed certain areas they should search. It was agreed that Maura would do most of the computer work. While they weren't sure if Devon had been detected, it wasn't a good idea to take a chance. Devon had no problems with that as long as he was kept in the loop.

He walked to the door with Conner.

"You will not go play on your computer."

A statement not a question. "I promise."

Conner gave him a look that told Devon he didn't believe that comment.

"Just stay off any searches that would lead to Ali. Do anything that's normal for you. If you are being monitored, we want them to think nothing has changed. The story has been filtered out through the club that Micah's worried about the baby, so you came home early."

"Some semblance of the truth is always the best."

Conner chuckled. "True. Don't hesitate to call me. If there is someone behind this, he or she killed a man of great value to the security systems, not only in the UK but to ours also. I want to nail this bastard."

He nodded and closed the door. When he turned, he found Kaheaku standing behind him. He stood there, his hands in his pockets, looking as if he hadn't a care in the world. Devon wasn't fooled. His cool green eyes took in everything. There was no doubt in Devon's mind that Kaheaku could kill him if he made a wrong move.

"We need to talk," Kaheaku said.

Devon inwardly stifled a groan. He wanted Kaheaku gone. Apparently that wasn't going to happen until he had his say.

"Let's go," Devon said.

He didn't look behind him as he walked down the hall to his study. Stepping in, he walked to his desk and sat down. He waited for Kaheaku to shut the door and take one of the two seats in front. When he didn't say anything, Devon decided to get the ball rolling.

"Have your say."

Kaheaku said nothing for a long moment. "Alicia has been on her own for a while now, but I feel that I should be watching out for her."

"Why is that?"

"Her father is gone and, without any kind of family around, I think she needs someone to make sure she isn't taken advantage of."

"I don't think she would appreciate you doing this."

Sean's lips twisted. "Probably not."

It bothered him that Kaheaku knew Ali better than he did. He knew there was nothing sexual between the two of them. All you had to do was be in the same room with the two of them. There was no sexual chemistry. But, they had a history that had been irritating him...along with one question.

"Answer me this, why didn't you worry about her before?"

"I did. I looked for her after Walter died. I heard about the explosion and for a while, they believed it was her." He sighed. "I already had my own issues at the time, and when it actually happened, I was in deep undercover in...well, let's not talk about that."

"Once you did hear?"

Kaheaku shook his head. "I never believed it. Walter, yes, but Alicia? That woman was raised to be a Teflon cat. She lands on her feet without much damage. I think MI-6 knew it wasn't her. Her DNA was on file."

"Why would they let people believe it was her?"

"Two reasons. One would be they might assume someone was after her. Because of her family, Alicia was well known in the organization. If she were alive, she was finding out who was after her. Sending out feelers could end with her death, so why mess with her."

"And if someone wasn't after her?"

"They would assume she was dirty and had decided to disappear. Best for them because of the embarrassment. If Walter and Alicia—two of their most trusted spies from their most trusted spy family—were to be found out to be dirty, that would be bad. Very bad."

It was his turn to study Sean. "Her own people would turn on her?"

Sean snorted. "You were with the Company. You know what those bastards are like."

"Yeah. But I don't know why you think I should have anything to do with you now?" He couldn't help but still feel a twinge of jealousy. Sean knew more about her and her life than Devon did. Apparently, the security expert picked up on it.

Sean rolled his eyes. "I'm not competition. That would be almost incestuous. I saw her as a little sister."

That didn't make him feel any better. "And?"

He stood and paced around the room. His movements were so out of character, Devon knew something was bothering him.

"You don't know how it was for her."

"Explain."

"Her father loved her, but he was fanatical about training her. When other girls were having sleepovers, Alicia was running drills. It wasn't easy for her."

"Okay."

"I thought he would never slip up. He was a legend in the business. I think both the CIA and KGB had studied him over the years. There was no situation he couldn't get out of. Or at least, I thought there wasn't. And when she disappeared right after her father died, I looked for her like I said. When I couldn't find her, I feared the worst. Little did I know she made one mistake."

"And that would be?"

Sean stopped pacing. "You."

Devon said nothing to that. He couldn't because he didn't like being anyone's mistake. Although...now that he thought of it, if a mistake was the best night of his life, he would gladly call himself a mistake.

"Oh, good lord, stop looking like that. It's disgusting."

Devon focused on Kaheaku again. "What?"

"I'm trying to have a conversation with you here, Stryker. You're getting all moony eyed and, damn, you're sweating."

He wasn't, was he? Now that he thought about it, it was kind of hot in his office.

"Sorry. Go on."

Sean collapsed in the chair he had vacated just a few moments earlier.

"She never had a boyfriend, you know. I'm pretty sure her first time in bed was on the job."

That cooled his libido. "Are you trying to tell me that she lost her virginity *on* the job?"

Sean nodded. "I don't like to think about it, mainly because it kind of grosses me out."

"Really?"

"Answer me this, Stryker. Do you want me to go into the last time I saw your sister and her husband put on a demonstration at Rough 'n Ready?"

He shook his head. "Point taken."

"She made a mistake with you. She should have just taken you down. The woman is lethal with her hands. A lot of people don't know that, but she is. She is almost always armed. Her father taught her well. And if she wanted to get information out of you right off, she could have interrogated you and gotten what she wanted. Instead, she ended up sleeping with you. Worse, she let you slip away."

"She was using me."

"You don't know much about the spy business, so I'll let you in on a little secret. A honey trap is a long kind of job. It's one way to gain the trust of the subject. Sometimes, it takes weeks to work. That was not what she should have been doing."

He shrugged. "She made a mistake."

"Yes, and if there is one person who knows how to work strategy, it would be Alicia. She should have known not to do that. She had one night...you don't go through with sex if you have them cornered. She had you cornered. Just know this, Stryker, you hurt her, I'll make sure they can't identify your remains."

"Is that a threat?"

The smile Kaheaku gave him had nothing to do with humor. "I don't issue threats, Stryker. I do offer promises, however."

"Understood."

"Do you know what your intentions are?"

"My main intention is to keep her and my child safe."

"I guess I can't ask you about after, because at the moment, there are too many variables."

He knew he could let it lie at that, but Devon decided to clear the air completely.

"Know this, I plan on making sure that both Ali and Bridget are safe but after, I do not plan on disappearing. Whether Ali likes it or not, I am sticking around for the next few decades."

ALICIA FOUND herself at loose ends. With Bridget gone, she didn't know what to do with herself. She had been honest with Devon. Since bringing Bridget home from the hospital, Alicia had never spent a night apart from her. She had been gone for less than half a day and she had talked to her daughter four times, and Dee had sent her at least a dozen pictures of the girls playing.

She walked down the stairs. Her life had changed so much over the years, but now she realized how much her own identity was wrapped up in her child. It wasn't something that bothered her, and she didn't regret it one bit.

Still, she was going to have to learn how to deal with being alone at some point. She heard the tapping of keys and realized that Devon was at work. She didn't really want to bother him.

Now, that's a lie, Ali girl.

She sighed as her father's voice filtered through her brain. If there was one person who knew her, it had been her father. And sadly, there things that she hid from him. Alicia wanted something. She wanted to ask Devon questions, but she was afraid of the answers. Right now she seemed to be missing the courage to face them.

I trained you better than that.

"Oh, bugger off."

The tapping stopped and she realized she had said the words out loud. She truly was losing her head.

"Ali?" Devon said from his office.

She stepped away from the direction of the office, but the floor creaked beneath her feet.

She heard his chair move, so she decided to face the music. When she stepped into the office, she was stunned at the size of it.

"This house keeps surprising me."

"What do you mean?"

"I didn't expect it to be so huge."

"Hawaii isn't known for them, but the builder had a lot of money. Then, the recession hit so I got this at a steal. Granted, most Hawaii real estate is going up, but this guy was at the end of his financial rope."

He watched her as she walked around the room. "Is there something you needed?"

She shook her head looking at the pictures. Nothing too old, but lots of them with Dee and her family, then some with Evan and other people.

"You have a nice network of friends."

He said nothing and she turned around. "Friends?" he asked.

She shrugged. "I never had that many because we lived all over the world. Well, until my cousin moved in with us."

"Why did he do that?"

"She. Her parents died. We were her only family, so father and mum took her in. She's a couple years older than I am."

He said nothing, just kept watching her. Guarded. He guarded all his thoughts around her. It irritated her even though she did the same thing.

"What about college?" he asked.

She shrugged. "I didn't go."

"Well, I didn't either."

"Father said I would be bored and he was probably right." Although, she had wanted to go. She had wanted the fun that Millicent was having. Parties, boys, learning for the first time outside of her father's instruction.

"I guess I should let you get back to work."

He shook his head. "I'm done for now. I was taking care of some emails. I also put your name in a database search engine I have. I want to see if anyone has been looking for you."

"There's someone, that's for sure."

He nodded. "But I mean *still*. If they search for you here, it would set off some alarm bells. Right now, they think you're in Washington. Or at least on the mainland."

She nodded but couldn't think of anything to say.

"Why don't you tell me why you're wandering around the house?"

"I don't know what to do."

"You don't let her stay over many nights?"

"Since we came from the hospital."

He opened his mouth, then it snapped shut. "Didn't your cousin..."

She shook her head. "When I say no one knew where I was, I was serious. My cousin has no idea where we are. That was for her protection as well as ours."

"Tell you what. Why don't we get some wine and go watch the sunset?"

It sounded romantic and very tempting. She hadn't had

much romance in her life, and definitely not the last few years.

"You don't have to entertain me, Devon."

His lips curved and when he spoke his voice dipped an octave lower. "Good, then you can entertain me."

He stood and stretched. His back made cracking noises. "Damn, I sat there too long. I could definitely do with some wine."

He walked passed her and grabbed her hand as he did. She had no choice but to follow him. And he was right. Relaxation might just bring her head back to where it needed to be.

sixteen

Devon walked beside Ali and tried to remember the last time he'd been this nervous. It was probably high school. No, it had been the night when he first met her. So odd that this woman, one he should never trust and definitely should avoid, was the woman who pulled at him. Even his first love couldn't compare. Nothing did, and that scared the hell out of him.

"You don't live here all the time, so where else do you live?" she asked.

"I have a flat in London."

He sensed her glance. Devon was glad when she didn't ask him about that. He didn't want to explain why he kept a flat there. Part of it was work, but it would be just as easy to rent some place or stay at a hotel. He had pegged her for someone from Great Britain. That had driven him to get a flat there. And now that he was thinking it, he was even more embarrassed. He had told himself at the beginning she had nothing to do with it, but now, with her here, he knew she did. It was kind of pathetic that he had gotten a flat with just the hope of running into her one day.

"I also keep that place in Vegas."

"Doesn't it get on your nerves?"

He felt his lips curve. "At times."

"Then why do you stay?"

"It's familiar and I like the anonymity of it."

She didn't respond, but he sensed that she didn't like his answer. He was lying of course, but he couldn't tell her the real reason he stayed in Vegas. Several times, he'd thought of moving back to the East coast, or making the permanent shift to Hawaii. He found himself unable to move away. The reason was walking beside him.

He had hoped one day she would return. He hadn't realized it until he saw her in Seattle, but he hadn't moved away because he hoped she would just appear again. He'd wanted to walk out to the bench that gave the best views of the sunset, but he decided to stay closer to the house.

"This house is fabulous."

"I like it. I was going to buy a condo, but I found this. The owner was very motivated to sell."

She sipped her wine and looked out across his lawn. "I particularly like the cannons."

He chuckled. "Yeah, like almost everything else, they came with the house."

She nodded and said nothing else. He wanted to demand to know what she was thinking. The truth was that the only person he knew more guarded than Ali was himself. He rarely let people into his inner circle easily. Hell, right now only a handful of people knew where he lived most of the time. And that would be cut in half if he didn't have contact with Dee.

"You think too much."

He turned to her. "Have you heard of the saying of the pot calling the kettle black?"

She chuckled. "Touché."

Then nothing.

It was an awkward silence. At least for him. He had so many questions he didn't even know where to start. He needed those answers to be happy, but there was something holding him back. Maybe he was a little too afraid of what she would say.

He needed answers. No, he needed to touch. The last few days had been stressful to say the least, but this had nothing to do with blowing off steam. From the moment he'd met her, Ali had gotten under his skin. He studied her. She was almost five years older, but it hardly showed. He liked the darker hair. It brought out those amazing eyes of hers. Her skin was just as luminous as before and—he sniffed—she smelled the same.

"Did you just smell me?"

He realized he had done just that and quite loudly. He could come up with something smart to say...if there was any blood left in his brain. It was rushing toward his groin. His cock strained against the zipper of his shorts.

She was smiling at him and he knew she had him. Right then, he would give everything he owned to touch her.

"Yes. I used to wake up in the middle of the night thinking I could smell you there."

She stopped smiling. The air between them seemed to

grow hotter and thicker. Her tongue darted out over her fuller, bottom lip. Her eyes darkened, dilated.

His cock hardened, pushing hard again. As his body heated, his heart doubled in speed.

"It wasn't as bad as the memory of tasting you. Do you know what makes me think of slipping my tongue into your hot, wet pussy?"

Ali shook her head slowly.

"Nothing. The truth is, nothing compares to it. I've been to some of the most celebrated bakeries in France...in the world. Nothing tasted so fucking good."

He closed his eyes and hummed. He hadn't been lying. He could taste her there, still. The flavor of her arousal danced over his taste buds even today.

When he opened his eyes, she was still staring at him. The pulse in her neck was erratic and fast.

"It is like pure sin wrapped in sugar."

She sucked in a breath and her face flushed. He knew just how sensual she was, but the fact that she blushed because of his description was an aphrodisiac. It pushed him to tease her more.

"Are your nipples hard, Ali?"

Devon didn't wait for an answer. He leaned forward and pressed his mouth against hers. As he did, he grazed the tip of one of her nipples with the backs of his fingers. Ali shivered and opened her mouth.

Now, he wanted her. He rose and pulled her to her feet, taking her empty glass and set it on the counter. She stopped him and he wanted to growl.

"Maybe we shouldn't be doing this."

"Maybe?" he asked, pulled her closer and kissing her again. She opened her mouth immediately, her tongue tangling with his.

"Yes. Things go wrong when we get together," she said against his mouth.

"Oh, no. Things go very, very right."

She moaned as he sucked on her tongue.

"Devon."

He pressed his groin against her. He was hard and getting harder by the moment. He wanted her...no needed her. It was just like that night years earlier. Something hot and dark moved through him, urging him to take her right there.

He pulled back then lifted her up on the counter.

"Devon?"

He ignored her. Instead, he pulled her panties off and leaned down. The scent of her arousal filled his senses. He placed a hand on each of her thighs and pushed them apart. The moment he set his mouth against her pussy, he was in heaven. Hot, intoxicating and amazingly like the night so many years earlier, he found himself lost in her. Her exotic taste danced over his taste buds as he slipped his tongue up and over her clit. Without warning she screamed his name, bucking against his mouth. He lapped at her juices, enjoying the way she pressed her hands against the back of his head. She leaned back, widened her legs and rode herself against his mouth to another orgasm.

He pulled back, stood and cursed. Then he spotted his wallet on the counter behind her. He fumbled with it, dropping it twice before he finally got the condom out. She was clawing at his pants, undoing them for him. He thanked the gods that he decided to go commando.

Ali tried to rush him by trying to grab the condom out of his hands. He batted them way and she growled. He slipped it down his cock, but she was attempting to help him. Her small touches almost had him coming right there. Devon slapped at her hands.

"Oy."

He looked up at her and laughed at the irritated expression on her face. That, along with the British slang, was so uncharacteristic he couldn't help but laugh more.

"I'm glad I amuse you," she said, annoyance threading her voice even as arousal deepened it.

"Oh, it's more than that, Ali. You make me so fucking happy."

The disgruntled expression dissolved into something more vulnerable. It wrapped around his heart and squeezed so fucking hard he almost passed out. That tough layer she presented to the world was peeling back, bit by bit. It was at that moment, he remembered why he fell for her. Remembered the way she had looked at him that night. It made him feel invincible...and it had made him think he had found the one woman who would understand him. In this one instant, he knew this was Ali, bare and undecorated with the years of training. Nothing artificial, nothing to hide her true feelings. This was the woman he wanted, the woman he would kill for.

Before she could collect herself and draw back, he leaned forward to brush his mouth over hers.

He pulled her hips closer so she sat on the edge of the

counter. He gyrated his hips, rubbing his penis along her dripping slit. Devon teased them both, allowing the head of his cock to brush up against her clitoris once or twice. She shifted, trying to change position to get him to penetrate her, but he placed a hand on her stomach.

Then, when neither of them could take it anymore, he drew back and entered her in one hard, quick thrust. He stayed there, not moving for a long minute or two. Wet warmth wrapped around his cock. He shuddered as everything came back to him just like before. He'd had good sex, but with Ali, it was hard to explain. Something was different...something made him feel as if he belong.

Slowly he pulled almost all the way out of her, then slid back in again. Damn. He didn't increase his pace. He wanted her with him. He wanted all her inner muscles moving over his cock as she came.

Each time he thrust into her, he sunk deeper...then deeper. She matched him in rhythm, raising her hips off the counter. Her moans rose in volume as both of them drew closer and closer to completion.

When he thought he couldn't hold back any longer, he took her mouth in a hot, wet, long kiss. Then, with his lips still on hers, he said, "Come with me, Ali."

He thrust once more and surrendered. She was there with him, chanting his name over and over as they both gave into pleasure.

LONG MOMENTS LATER, Ali became aware of her surroundings. She shifted. She was laying on something very hard and cold. She opened her eyes.

Good God, she made love on the kitchen island. She wasn't inhibited, but...she still had her sundress on and Devon was still dressed. She was lying on top of the counter as Devon lay on top of her. He was still standing, but he was snuggled up to her chest.

"Devon."

"Hmm?" He didn't say anything else, but he did nibble on her neck. The small action had her head spinning. What the bloody hell was the man doing to her?"

"We're on the kitchen island."

He nibbled his way up to her earlobe. "Yeah we are."

"And the doors are open and we're unprotected."

It took him a second. He gave her lobe one last nip then straightened away. When he looked down at her, he was smiling. But after a few seconds, his smile faded.

"What?"

He shook his head. "I like you like this."

"Ravished on your kitchen island?"

"I like you here. I like you with me. Better, I like myself when I'm with you."

She found it hard to breathe. She had never had a man talk to her like that before. On the job, her assignments tried everything to seduce, capture her. Most of the men she'd come in contact with had been accustomed to big gestures. Simple words...honest words. Those were rare, but Devon had no problem with that.

She sat up and kissed him. "I like the way I am with you too."

His mouth curved up on one side. Bloody hell, she loved this man. It wasn't something she wanted right now, but in the depths of her mind, she knew she needed it. Needed him. For more than protection.

And that scared the bloody hell out of her.

"What?"

She shook her head and tried to kiss him, but he stopped her.

"Honesty."

She sighed. He was demanding it. Worse, she wanted to give it to him. In all her life, she had been honest with only two people. Her father and her daughter. Now, this man who had changed the course of her life, given her the one thing that made her complete, wanted something from her.

"I'm a wee bit overwhelmed by you. By my feelings."

His smile was lopsided. "That makes two of us, love."

She nodded.

He stepped back from her and locked the doors, set the alarm and before she could jump down from the counter, he picked her up.

"Wait, Devon, I'm too heavy."

"Why do women always say that? You barely weigh anything."

He carried her up the stairs and into his bedroom. She hadn't been in there before, but she had peeked in. It had the best view out of all the rooms, with a lanai off the other side of the massive king sized bed. The bay sparkled in the moonlight. The colors were bold and masculine, rich with greens and dark browns. She thought he would head to the bed, but he bypassed it and headed to the bathroom. He set her on the counter there, then stripped out of his clothes.

God, he was gorgeous. If anything, he'd improved his physique the last few years and he'd matured. There was a smattering of hair on his chest and a thin trail down his abs.

His cock was hard again, curving up against his stomach. She couldn't resist. She slipped her hand over the long length of his penis. It jerked against her hand.

"You keep doing that, I'm not going to last that long."

She looked at him. "Is that a fact?"

He nodded. "Besides, I want you naked first, then I want you in that shower," he said, motioning with his head behind him.

There was enormous Egyptian shower behind him, with a long ledge against the back wall of it. There were two show-erheads.

He pulled off her dress, tossing it aside with little notice from either of them. Cool air washed over her heated flesh.

"Damn."

His gaze focused on her breasts. Brushing the backs of his fingers over one nipple, he sighed.

"I like all that sexy lace you wore before but this..." He didn't finish his sentence. Instead, he leaned down and took the nipple into his mouth. He sucked it into his mouth with such force she moaned. It hurt a bit, but the pleasure out did the pain he had caused. He pinched and teased the other nipple as he grazed his teeth over the one he already had in his mouth.

Soon she couldn't take it anymore. Alicia pushed on his

shoulders and he relented. He stepped back, opened the shower, turning on both of the heads, then scooped her up off the counter. Before stepping in, he doubled back and opened a drawer to grab a condom. He set her in the shower and shut the door behind them. The water was lukewarm but she didn't care. He set the condom on the soap dish, turned and backed her against the wall. The kiss he gave her was wanton and delicious. Again and again, he thrust his tongue into her mouth. It was a blatant assault on her senses and she loved it. But she was sick of being taken. She wanted to be a participant.

Alicia pressed her hands on his shoulders and after one last, long suck on his tongue, she pushed him back away from her. Without a word, she slid down to her knees in front of him. His cock dripped with water and droplets of precum wet the bulbous head.

Wrapping one hand around him, she stroked his cock, teasing the head with a swipe of her thumb. A quick drawn in breath was the only response he had to it. She looked up as she continued to move her hand over his hardened flesh. He was watching her hand, then his gaze moved to hers. She leaned forward and took just the head of his cock into her mouth. The sweet/salty taste of his cum danced over her taste buds. She wanted to make him lose control and pour himself into her mouth and throat.

With that in mind, she ramped up her attack. She took him fully in her mouth, as his hands settled on the back of her head. He fucked her face, pushing his cock so far back into her mouth she almost gagged. With delight, she slid her tongue over his hardened flesh. She slipped her hands around to his rear and pressed against him. He was groaning and she thought for sure he would come, but he pulled away with a curse.

She blinked trying to get her focus back. When he reached over to grab the condom his hands were shaking. He fumbled with the wrapper but he got it open and slipped it on. Then, he pulled her up to her feet. The shower spun around her as he reversed their positions.

"Bend over," he ordered.

She turned around to tell him she didn't like his tone, but he smacked her on her ass. The sound of wet flesh against his palm filled the room. That should have outraged her, but the sting filtered out over her rear end. He smacked her again, this time a little harder. The pleasure/pain shot straight to her pussy this time. Bloody hell.

"Don't fuck with me right now." The threat in his voice scared and aroused her. She bent over and rested her weight on her hands on the ledge.

He took her by the hips and entered her from behind. It was hard, fast, and she couldn't seem to keep up. Apparently, Devon didn't care. Again and again he entered her, so hard she almost fell over a few times. He let loose a frustrated growl and turned them around. He was still inside of her as he pressed her against the glass of the shower. She put her hands on the glass to steady herself.

Devon slid his hands around to her breasts, his fingers digging into her delicate flesh. It hurt, but she didn't care. All she cared about was coming. Thrust after thrust, he pushed her closer.

"Fuck," Devon said. He continued to slam against her. She was beyond any kind of rational thought at that point.

One moment she was dying for relief and in the next, her orgasm exploded within her. Relief danced over her nerve endings as she bucked and convulsed. It was as if she had broken through some kind of barrier. Before she was done with the first, she fell into another even more powerful orgasm. This one shattered her. She broke apart in a million little pieces of delight as she screamed so loud the echo of her voice hurt her ears.

"Oh, yeah, fuck, that's it," Devon muttered as he continued to thrust in and out of her.

But he wasn't done. He changed his angle and continued on. He pushed her over the edge so many times; she lost all sense of time. Finally, when she felt she would dissolve if she had another release, she had one more. With a shout, he followed her, pumping into her.

He fell back and sat on the ledge, pulling her with him. He set his head against her back. She couldn't even think, couldn't come up with words, so she leaned back against him and just let the water cascade over both of them.

seventeen

Alicia woke when she felt Devon's lips moving over her back. His tongue darted out over her flesh every now and then. She smiled.

"Well, that's a nice way to wake up," she murmured. And it was. She had never laid about in bed with a lover in this way. There was no deception, no one listening. It was just them. Just like the night they met. Was that why she found him so special? She'd never shared a private moment before Vegas and this was even more precious. Now, they knew where both of them were coming from and there was no lying.

It was if she had been virgin when she went to bed with him.

"I have all kinds of interesting ways to wake you up."

His voice was gruff and deep, filled with arousal.

She looked behind her. He was on his hands and knees on the bed. His hair was a mess and there was a day's growth on his chin. How was it fair that men could look a mess and still be attractive?

"What are you thinking?"

She smiled and turned back around. "I'm wondering who you've been practicing these moves on."

There was a beat of silence and he stilled, then he started moving his mouth over her back again.

"I did not practice on anyone."

"So, you've been celibate since our night?" she asked, actually amused by the banter.

If she wasn't trying to gain some kind of information from a man, she didn't know how to flirt. And, being fair, she couldn't judge him for what he did in their years apart.

"I'm sure this is the first time you've had sex in four years," he said, a bit of sarcasm lacing his words.

She sighed as he started to use his hands along with his mouth. The kitchen counter had been hard on her back.

"It is."

Without warning, he flipped her over onto her back. Then, he loomed over her.

"What do you mean?"

She slipped her hands up over his shoulders. "It's not like I had a lot of time to cruise bars."

And truthfully, she didn't know the first thing about dating. Her first time had been on a mission, the whole thing recorded.

His eyes narrowed. "You have to have a string of lovers."

She frowned. "No. I had targets."

Something she couldn't discern moved over his expression. "So, it's been four years?"

She nodded and felt a shiver of fear and arousal inter-twine as it moved through her blood. The dangerous look on his face should scare her, but there was a part of her that found it thrilling. All that attention, focused on her.

"I guess we have to make up for some lost time."

And with that, he kissed his way down her body, grazing his teeth over her flesh. She pushed her present worries out of her mind as she gave herself over to his expert touch.

"I'M STARVING," Devon said. Ali giggled. Actually giggled. He never thought he would hear such a sound come from the woman. It made him so fucking out happy to hear. "I'm not joking."

"It's not my fault we didn't eat dinner," she said, sitting up and, unfortunately, pulling the sheet up. "You're the one who said he could live on sex."

He chuckled when he remembered his announcement earlier that day. "I'll give you that."

She smiled down at him and in that minute, he knew he was lost to her. Her hair was a tangled mass of curls dripping over her shoulders, her lips were swollen from his kisses, and she had that kind of glow from a good healthy bout of passion.

Shit. He was falling in love with her. Not knee deep, either. He was head first, going under for the third time in love with her. He had to have been in love with her a little that night four years ago, but this was something more.

Her smile dimmed. "What?"

Devon used to be better at hiding his feelings. But something about Ali always tugged at his emotions, pulling them out into the open. He wanted to tell her everything, but he couldn't. They needed time to process, to come to terms with what they were dealing with—and there was a little girl involved.

So, instead, he decided to keep it light. "You know you're kind of ugly, right?"

She laughed. "Is that so?"

He nodded. "You kind of smell too."

She shook her head. "I know when I'm not wanted."

Turning, she started to crawl out of bed, but he grabbed her again, tumbling them over the sheets. He pressed her body into the mattress with his.

"Where do you think you're going?" he asked.

"I thought maybe I would find some food."

He sighed as he felt his body respond to her, but he knew she was right. They needed food. He gave her a quick kiss then rolled off her and the bed. He grabbed a t-shirt and tossed it to her.

"Thank you," she said so primly he laughed. "What?"

"Nothing. You are a contradiction in terms. So ladylike and proper now, but I think I have scratches on my back."

Her face flushed and he thought back to what Kaheaku said...and her own confessions. The idea that she had never really dated boggled his mind. This was a new experience for her. And he was the one to give it to her.

He grabbed a pair of boxers and stepped into them. "Let's go see what we can find."

He held his hand out as an invitation. She stared at it as if it was a foreign entity. It took her only a moment longer to respond. She stood and took his hand. It wasn't a huge step, but a significant one. He raised their joined hands to his mouth and kissed her knuckles without taking his gaze from hers.

Then, he led her downstairs.

WHEN ALICIA POLISHED off her bowl of ice cream, she licked the spoon dry.

"I don't think I've ever been this hungry, except for the last trimester I was pregnant with Bridget."

"You were on your own?" he asked.

"Yes. I didn't have anyone I could call on, so I decided to play the role of single mother."

"And you were one."

Alicia looked up at him and saw the genuine interest in his gaze. She nodded. "It was scary. I had gone to South Africa to have her."

He frowned. "Why there?"

"My mother's family had some land there and it wasn't really tied to us. I have a fake identity I could use. I'm pretty damned good with the accent."

"And no one knew about it?"

She shook her head. "Although about three months after having Bridget, I had to move. I had a few inquiries from someone about who I was. I didn't stick around to find out who it was."

"Smart."

She tried not to get so happy about his approval. "I am my father's daughter."

"So, you looked for me?" he asked. "When you felt you had to run from South Africa?"

"Not then. I'd become paranoid. But when I found out I was pregnant, I did look for you. It's a good thing I didn't find you or I would have never moved back to the states."

"Why?"

"I thought you had something to do with my father's death. I wasn't about to let you within ten feet of Bridget."

"And you didn't think I should know about her?"

She sighed as the emotions from those days washed over her. The panic, the fear...the horror that she was alone in the world.

"I didn't know. I wasn't in my right mind. Pregnancy...it zaps your brain cells. Losing my father shattered me, then knowing I had this little being to protect...I started to under-stand why my father was so fanatical about my safety. And I had a few close calls while I was pregnant. I tried to hang around Paris, but I barely made it out of there alive."

"And still you didn't come find me."

"If I had known this is who you were, I would have tracked your fertile ass down and demanded you help."

His lips twitched. "Fertile ass?"

"Yes. Bloody hell, I was on the pill and we used a condom. Ending up pregnant was kind of beyond anything statistics could predict. But, not knowing what the hell was going on, I couldn't chance it. Having the attack at my own house...that was over the top. It was the one place I knew we were always safe."

His frown darkened. "And the bastard knew it. Which means he knew you."

She nodded. "I know I can't do anything to make up for the time you lost with Bridget, but I just want you to understand that I had no choice. I didn't know where to turn and I couldn't trust anyone's information."

"What about Kaheaku?"

"Sean?"

He nodded.

"I didn't think of him. No, that's not true. I did think of him, but I had no way of contacting him. When he started working in private contracting, he wasn't the easiest to find. Add to that the threat...I just couldn't involve him. I had a very real fear that anyone connected to me would end up in danger. Sean would be pissed to know that I was trying to protect him, but I had to."

He said nothing for a moment, then he reached out with his hand and cupped her face.

"You're tough, you know that?"

She tried to shake his hand away by moving her face, but he refused.

"No. I want you to know that in any fight, I'd want you at my back. I trust you, but know that you don't have to do this alone anymore. I'm here and there are people who want to help."

Tears stung the backs of her eyes. She blinked trying to keep them from falling, but she failed. He wiped them away with the backs of his fingers, then leaned over to kiss her. It was more sweet than carnal, but it affected her more than any kiss he'd offered her before. In this, she felt his dedication and trust. He pulled back and rested his forehead on hers.

"I owe my sister a big gift."

She smiled. "Why is that?"

"She's the one who talked Micah and me into going to Seattle. As soon as the dust settles, she'll remember and won't shut up about it."

She chuckled and was about to suggest they go back upstairs, but his mobile rang.

"Hey, Conner."

She moved away from him, but he grabbed her hand and kept her standing beside him.

"Shit. Yeah, I know that name."

He was quiet for a few seconds, and took the opportunity to kiss her knuckles.

"When?" Another silence. "I'll see when you get here."

He hung up and looked at her. She knew there was something pretty bloody important if Conner was coming over right away at this time of night.

"Do you know anything about the Spencer File?"

She cocked her head to the side and thought. Then the stories came flooding back to her and she smiled. "Oh, that. It's an urban fantasy."

He didn't smile. "Tell me."

"There was a rumor about a spy who had sold information to some of our enemies. The problem was that it seemed to pop up whenever we had a mission go bad without explanation. I remember early on in my career, we had one big bloody fuck up, but sometimes it is just a coincidence or someone slipped somewhere. So many of us are guarded all the time, but it just takes one little slip—a drunken confession, something like that. So, in the end it isn't true. It's used to scare agents I think."

Devon shook his head. "No. The Spencer File was pretty damned real, because I was the one who discovered it and brought it to the attention of the CIA and MI-6."

"Wait. This went back too many years to be one person. That's why it was always dismissed."

"I had come up with some information, or at least a theory that it was a network of double agents who were recruited by the others already working as a mole."

"But what does that have to do with my father?" she asked. "You're not suggesting that my father was a traitor are you?"

He shook his head. "No. Conner uncovered your father's files. I don't even want to know what laws Maura broke, but they found references to it. That's why he was looking for me. He needed help working on what he wanted to find out."

"Are you telling me my father read your file and wanted to connect with you about that?"

He nodded. "I think so. I also think it's what might have gotten him killed."

eighteen

By the time Conner got to the house, they had dressed. Alicia tried to calm her heart rate, but it was hard to do. Devon showed Conner into the office. Alicia could tell from his expression that it wasn't good news.

He shook his head and gave her an apologetic glance. "I hate to bother y'all this late at night, but we also got a hit right before I came over. Rory called with the information. Right now, I don't want to do any more talking over the phone."

She knew Rory was one of the head security specialists they employed and one of the few people who had known who she was.

"No problem. And I have to agree. Using the phone, no matter how secure, is always a security issue. Truth is, the sooner we figure all of this out, the sooner I can feel safe again."

The idea that she would finally be able to just live her life was a fantasy she'd never thought would come true. She'd been looking over her shoulder for so many years...and she wanted to be a regular mom to Bridget.

Conner pulled out his tablet, tapped on the screen a few times and brought up the files.

"So, what's this about the Spencer file?" she asked. "What did you find?"

"The Spencer File. Yes, well, I'd always thought it one of those rumors that were never going to be proven." He looked at Alicia with a hint of understanding in his eyes. "All spooks have that weird story of a spy selling secrets. Born and raised in the country they have been ordered to destroy. The big one here was of a Soviet being raised as an American."

"But it isn't a myth," Devon said. "Not from what I found."

"Exactly," Conner said grimly. "I didn't expect you to react like you did."

Devon nodded. "I remember that. I got a few laughs at the office when I went after it."

"Are you sure this was real? It had always been considered a boogie man kind of story for agents. Like to scare us into being good little spies," Alicia said. "I know my father dismissed it for years. But something changed his mind when he started to research old cases."

"I know it is. I had too many reliable sources not to believe them. Plus, when I presented the information, the higher ups got very quiet," Devon said. "It was a little eerie the way all contact was broken off from them."

"Oh, that's not good," she said. "When a spook goes silent, that's usually a very bad thing."

"Why did you latch onto it?" Conner asked.

Devon shrugged. "Not entirely sure. I've always been a geek and there were a lot of little places on the internet that chatted about it. The complexity of it intrigued me. Like a puzzle. The prevailing opinion was that they resurrected the name over and over to use. That it was a family kind of thing."

That made sense to her. In fact, it was a bit brilliant. "So, like Menudo?"

"What?" Conner asked. Devon was looking at her like she were insane.

"Like the boy band from Mexico. When a band member would get too old, they just replaced them with another boy. That way they kept it young and maintained teenager interest."

Devon smiled. "Odd, but yes, that's what they did. Or what I could discern. Maybe it was that fact that made it seem unbelievable. Since the rumors had been around more than twenty years, it seemed implausible. But what if the same people—or in this case country—used the name over and over, then that would make sense. It would seem that the spy never aged."

"Yes, and apparently, it was sent to England. It was their issue after all. And, that's where your father comes in, Alicia."

"I'm seeing where this is going. The CIA handed it over and nothing was done right away. They let it sit there for a few years, but my father was semi-retired. His mind was as sharp as ever, and he had the right security clearance. He'd been going over old information, looking at missions that went right, those that went wrong, and writing up reports. I think he said something about using them for training. Father was one of the few agents around who could remember some of those days and he still held his security clearance. So, this must have hit his desk."

Conner hit a few things on his tablet then handed it to them. "This is apparently where he got, and Devon's name came up."

He handed it to Devon and he shared the screen with her. The file was American in origin and Devon's name was blacked out.

"How did he find out it was you?" She rolled her eyes. "He called someone. Dad knew someone in every bloody spook agency around the world."

He nodded. "That's the report I made up on it. It was right before my life went to complete shit, so I completely forgot about it."

Conner's mobile rang. He answered.

"I told you I wanted to stay off the phone for security." He rolled his eyes and listened to whoever was on the phone.

"Okay." He handed the phone to Devon. "It's Rory. He wants to talk to you about this report. He can only find what I have there and he wants to know if you remember anything."

Devon took the phone and moved away from them to talk.

Alicia glanced at the clock and realized it was probably before sunrise in Florida. "I hate that Rory is up this early working, but I really appreciate it."

Conner gave her a sardonic smile. "First, I always like

bugging Rory. He's involved with my sister and well, I like screwing with him. Plus, he's on Miami time so it's not *that* early."

She nodded then continued to look through the report, noting some of the sources. Then, there was a name that stood out amongst the notes.

Xan Winslow.

A chill ran down her spine, seeping into her soul. All the moisture seemed to evaporate in her mouth and she found it hard to swallow.

What a bloody, bloody mess. All the sounds around her seemed to fade away and she felt the room spin. She gathered up enough strength to draw in a deep breath. She realized then that Conner was still talking.

"And, someone has a huge hard-on for you, Alicia. They've been looking for you the last few weeks; I pinpointed their traveling IP. They were on the west coast, but the latest is Honolulu."

"Here?"

Her heart almost stopped right then and there.

"Yes. In fact, they're staying down in Waikiki, although we haven't been able to pinpoint it exactly. The closest we could get is three blocks. But my bet is whoever they are, they are staying at one of the hotels."

She would be able to contact the traitor. It was a number she'd avoided using in the past, but now, she would.

"Do you have any backup tonight?" Conner asked.

"Devon's here," she said, trying to come up with a way to get out of the house undetected.

"I mean for both of you. If you want, I can stay."

"When Devon gets done with Rory, we'll see what he says. Can you excuse me for a moment?"

He nodded and she slipped out of the room. As she walked up the stairs, her mind started racing. She should have known something was going on. Every turn in the case had been reported by one person. The one person she thought she had been protecting.

Other people would never catch on to who it was. In fact, she might be the only person alive who could connect all the dots. The name was the giveaway. She dressed as fast as she could. She grabbed her Glock and strapped her knife holder to her ankle. After grabbing her knife, she slipped it into the holder. She turned toward the door, but she stopped. There was only one person on her mind for so long, now she had two.

Both of them were in her heart and he needed to know how she felt. And she needed to provide for her daughter.

She grabbed a piece of paper and wrote down a few words, explaining what she was doing and where she was going. And she did the one thing she thought she would never do before ending the note. She placed it on the dresser in plain sight, and this time, she slipped out down the stairs and out of the house.

AFTER GETTING OFF THE PHONE, Devon and Conner discussed the possibilities of who it could be. It would have to be someone her father knew and someone who was still around. That really narrowed the field, but not enough. After a while Devon realized it had been close to thirty minutes since Ali left the room.

Devon stepped out of the office.

"What's wrong?" Conner said as he followed him out.

Devon shook his head and walked up the stairs. The sense of urgency growing with each step he took. He made it to the top of the stairs and ran down to her room.

"Ali!" No answer. And no one in the room. He ran through the bathroom to the other bedroom and found it empty too.

He knew there had been something wrong, but he'd thought it was something else. She had been tired and all the information was a little too much for even him to take.

"Dev," Conner yelled. Devon ran back in and found Conner holding a piece of stationary.

He handed it over and pulled out his phone.

DEVON,

Well, it's my turn to run. This is my fight not yours. It was never yours. I know that now. My father had only looked at your research to know the person responsible for this problem.

I am leaving this note for you. And, there is information in my safe deposit box and in my bag. It names you as the father of my child. Please, if I don't return from this, love her like I do. You are the only person I trust her to. Protect her. She is the most precious thing to me on this earth and beyond.

Love,

Ali

He looked up and found Conner hanging up this phone. "I talked to Sean since he knew them. There is one person that came to mind. Her cousin."

He shook his head trying to piece it all together.

"How did Sean know?"

"The first job he ever worked with MI-6 on a joint task force had one grating person, and that was Millicent Hughes. Her name on the job was Xan Winslow."

The name clicked. "Fuck."

"Exactly."

"At least I know she's not flying back to England."

Conner shook his head. His frown turned darker.

"No, Millicent is here. There was a hit from here on the island. I mentioned the hotel and I know Alicia. She's going to go after her."

She left him to go die. "And now we are. Let's go."

nineteen

Alicia had to fight the guilt that swamped her as she sped down H-3 on her way to Waikiki. She'd found it ridiculously easy to roll Devon's car down the driveway before turning it on and taking off. She waited until she knew Devon didn't follow her right away to call her cousin. She dialed the number, Millicent answered before the first ring finished.

"Alicia."

Her voice was warm but it chilled Alicia to the bone. Millicent had been waiting for her...lying in wait for her call. All these years Millicent had played a deep game. The idea that Alicia had thought Millicent was the one person she could trust...it almost made her stick to her stomach.

"Where are you?" she asked.

"No greeting? I thought you'd want to catch up."

Oh, she could see the sarcastic smile on her cousin's face. She always liked to think she was smarter than everyone else. Alicia had always ignored it, thinking it came from her need to belong to the family. Now, it was annoying the bloody hell out of her.

"Cut the shit, Millicent. I don't have time for it."

"So crass." She sighed dramatically over the phone. "I'm staying at a resort in Waikiki, but it is a bit too busy to meet."

She knew what that meant. "What you mean is that you don't want witnesses."

"Tsk, tsk, Ali. Don't you trust me?" The sickly sweet tone made Alicia sick.

"Don't call me that." It made her ill to think of Millicent using the nickname Devon and her father had used for her. "And of course I don't trust you. You killed my father."

"Be nice or I will have to dig deeper on why you had a little girl's room at your house in Seattle."

Her blood iced over. The first thing that came to her mind was to tell her cousin to go bugger herself, but she refused to lose it. With what Millicent had done so far, she probably wouldn't think twice about killing Bridget.

"Just tell me where to meet you."

Her cousin sighed again, but she finally rattled off an address.

"I'll be there. Not sure how long."

"You've got half an hour."

She clicked the phone off then turned on the GPS. She didn't need it until she got closer, but she knew that Devon would be looking for her by now. This way he could find her.

She stepped on the gas as she came through the mountain to the other side of the island.

DEVON CURSED when he found his car missing.

"Damned spook," he growled, making his way to Conner's car. He dialed his sister's number. Micah answered.

"What's up?"

"Is everything okay there?" he asked.

He heard the sheets rustling and Micah moving around. "I haven't heard a thing."

Then a slight pause and Devon had to pray for patience. He knew Micah was walking down the hall to Alana's room to check on Bridget.

"Girls are both asleep in bed," he whispered.

Devon released a breath he didn't know he had been holding.

"What's going on?" Micah asked.

"Ali found out who put this all in motion and then decided to run off to Waikiki to confront her."

"Well, you know how to pick them. Need me?"

He knew his brother-in-law would come without a second thought. Devon would trust Micah with his life, but he needed his brother-in-law to protect something much more important.

"I've got Conner with me. I'd rather you be there to protect Bridget. I'm not sure what they know about her."

"You got it."

He hung up the phone as Conner took off down H-3.

"Do you know where you're going?"

"I know that her cousin doesn't know the area and she was somewhere in Waikiki. It's late, but she isn't going to meet her at the hotel. At least this way we can keep an eye out for your car."

He nodded. The fact that she had stolen his car while he'd been sitting in the office discussing what they should do still pissed him off. She'd turned the tracker on his car and now she was speeding off to meet the woman who had killed her father.

"What about her phone? It's a long shot, but you never know."

He had gotten her a new phone when they left Seattle and it was on his plan. He punched in the number and it didn't come up right away. Then...it beeped. It showed her already on H-1 nearing Honolulu.

"You were right," he said. "Go into Waikiki."

Conner listened to his directions and said nothing else for a few minutes.

"You need to keep your temper so you don't cause any problems," he said finally.

He glanced at Conner then looked ahead. "I will, but when I get her alone after this, we're going to have a serious talk."

With each mile they covered, Devon's irritation grew. He could not believe the woman actually left him to handle it on her own. Running off in the middle of the night to face the woman who killed her father and put a hit out on Ali and Bridget.

Conner shook his head. "Being pissed now is going to make you stupid."

"I'm mad and I can use that. I know how to control it."

Conner said nothing as he made his way off H-1 and followed Devon's instructions to the park. They rolled to a stop behind his car. There was another car there, a rental. The GPS for her phone was still moving. He held it up and showed Conner. They both pulled out their guns and carefully got out of the car.

ALICIA SAW the light just when she was about to give up. Just as her cousin had said, she was sitting in a pavilion with a small overhead light above her head. As she approached her from the side, Alicia searched the landscape. She no longer trusted the bitch she considered her sister. Nothing stood out to her, but that didn't mean anything. She didn't know the terrain well. She just hoped her senses would be as sharp as they once were.

"There's no need to try and be quiet. I know you're out there."

Bloody hell. With a sigh, she stepped up on the cement and faced her cousin. Lord, she really didn't look good. Only a few years older, Millicent didn't age that well. Her hair was threaded with gray hair and was a mess. In fact, she looked like she hadn't washed it in days. While she was still in shape, her face showed the years. She looked at least ten years older than she was. She was also holding a pistol with a silencer.

Ali said nothing when faced with her cousin.

Always allow the bastard to do the talking. They always like to brag of their exploits, Ali girl.

It was hard to deal with the emotions now swamping her, but she bit her lip. She wanted to scream at the girl she had known. The one who had been her confidant, her best friend, and the person she told everything to. Until...her father's death. Something had told her to keep the truth from her. Maybe Ali has sensed the cold calculating bitch that lay beneath the façade.

"Oh, if you could see your expression," Millicent said, amusement dancing in her voice. "You look so hurt. What's the matter, Alicia, did you think we were friends?"

"No. We were family."

Millicent's humor faded. "Yes, your father said the same thing."

Just hearing that, knowing that her father had faced off with Millicent...and she still killed him, left a hollow feeling at the bottom of her stomach. She could only think of one question.

"Why?"

"Why what?" she asked in that sickly sweet tone again.

"Why did you have to sell secrets?"

"I guess you never suspected before now, did you?"

Alicia shook her head.

"My father didn't just die. He did the same thing as I did. He had to. Circumstances left him with no choice in the matter."

Ali had guessed someone had held the job before Millicent. "He was the first Xan."

"Correct. See, your father had all that money, but well,

mine had none. We suffered while your father and mother lived a lavish lifestyle."

They hadn't really had an extravagant life. The house had been willed to her mother and her father had lived off what he earned. They had always traveled but it had been for the job.

"They both had a trust...the same amount. Your father started out with as much money as mine."

Millicent shrugged. "Yes, well, father liked to live life to the fullest, as did my mother. We did have a lot of fun. Fun that always seemed to take so much money."

Glimpses of Millicent's parents with expensive cars, clothes...anything they could seem to get their hands on. Even as a child, she had been able to see the difference between the brothers.

Alicia shifted her weight on her feet and Millicent held her gun up. "Don't forget, I don't have a problem killing blood relatives."

She had guessed, but now she knew. "So that answers that."

Millicent leaned forward. Evil painted an ugly smile on her face. "Yes, I killed him, but I had no choice. He found me out and then he went on to tell me he would help me. Like your father would make sure I didn't go to prison."

She swallowed the lump in her throat. Of course her father would have done that. He would have seen that as his responsibility to help Millicent. And because of that, he was now dead.

"You were our family. You could have come to us for help. You didn't have to sell secrets."

A sound of disgust fell from her lips. "Yes, of course. Poor, little orphan Millicent being saved by the benevolent uncle and her perfect fucking cousin. That would be just brilliant."

"It wasn't like that."

Millicent tossed some of her stringy, greasy hair back. "Yes. It was. When I came to live with you, you never accepted me."

She searched through her memories, but could not come up with what her cousin was talking about. They had shared everything from clothes to secrets.

"We accepted you. We loved you."

"I know you pretended to, but there was always something missing. As if I wasn't truly one of the family. I always felt left out."

"And so you took him away from me?" she asked. Unable to hide the pain I her voice, it quivered.

"I'm sorry but are you missing the point—he was going to turn me over to be interrogated. He kept saying he would take care of me, make sure that I could be saved the jail time. I just had to turn secrets over to the British."

"He would have done it, and he had the power and contacts."

"I didn't want that. Don't you understand? I am sick to death of your father and you. So fucking bloody righteous, you two. Never did a thing out of line."

"You could have talked to me about it. I would have helped you."

"I think not, Alicia. Are you telling me you will save me?"

She opened her mouth, but Millicent wasn't going to listen. As her cousin stood and stepped closer, Alicia saw it there in her eyes. No empathy, no love...and just a little mad. The woman was not playing with a full stack.

Now or never, Ali girl. Take that little bitch down.

With her father's voice in her head, she reached behind her to grab the gun in her waistband. Her cousin was too quick. Before Alicia could raise her gun, Millicent shot her arm. The hot burn of the bullet forced her to drop the gun. She tumbled to the ground, her head hitting the pavement. She was stunned for a moment, but she rolled and swept her legs under Millicent's feet. Her cousin screamed as she tumbled to the ground. Fear and anger pumped through Alicia as she rose to her knees and went after her cousin.

Alicia balled up her fist and hit Millicent square in the nose. The sound of bone breaking left her slightly ill as blood spurted.

"You bitch," Millicent screamed.

She fought her way to her feet, and her cousin realized she'd lost her gun also. Alicia moved to grab her backup gun, when she felt cold metal against her temple.

"Oh, I have dreamed of this for years. I was disappointed that I gave up that Aston Martin and I didn't even kill you. The best part about all of this is that I will now have all your money."

Alicia almost opened her mouth to correct her. Bridget would inherit everything. Millicent thought she had succeeded in hiding herself from everyone. With the GPS, Devon and Conner would surely find her soon. Millicent would end up in jail, even if Alicia had to die to get her arrested.

"Stand up," Millicent ordered. She tugged her up by the shoulder of her shirt.

Alicia tried to think of a way to get to her knife, but with the gun aimed at her head, it was too much to risk. She held her hands up and got up to her feet. When she did, she saw a slight movement out of the corner of her eye. She prayed it was Devon and Conner or she truly was dead.

"Goodbye, Alicia. I really hate to have to do this."

Alicia refused to give up. She turned and faced her cousin. "Do it this way you cowardly, traitorous bitch."

Millicent's mouth tightened as she steadied her arm, leveling the gun at Alicia's heart. The second before she pulled the trigger, a shot rang out from the left. It hit Millicent square in the chest. She stumbled back and dropped her gun. Blood soaked the white shirt she was wearing.

She fell against the picnic table and then rolled down to the ground. It was as if she were watching some kind of horrible movie in slow motion. Pounding feet came rushing toward her.

Devon reached her first. He grabbed her and shook her until her teeth chattered.

"Don't you ever fucking do that again!" he yelled. She opened her mouth but found herself crushed against his chest. "Just don't."

"How is she?" Conner said.

"Fine."

She blinked, trying to focus on Conner's grim face. He walked over to Millicent and felt for a pulse.

"Is she alive?" she asked, but her voice sounded weak to her ears.

"No."

The sound of sirens grew as lights flooded the area. She tried to swallow and almost choked on bile. The area began to fly by her as if she were on a merry-go-round. She blinked again, trying to focus on something, anything.

"Devon."

"I don't want to hear it. I can't believe you left me like that."

"I don't want to fight about it. Not right now."

"That makes two of us."

"I do need one thing from you," she said, as uniformed officers filled the area.

"What's that?" he bit out.

"Don't let me fall."

Then she tumbled into a deep black hole.

twenty

Devon paced the hallway at Queen's Medical Center as they waited for Ali to be taken care of. Worst part was that they had refused to let him ride in the ambulance. He wasn't considered family so he'd been told to drive. Thankfully, Conner had shoved him in his car and driven him to the hospital. Now they waited.

He looked down at the scrubs he now wore. They were pale blue, faded from many washings. The officer who met them at the hospital had taken his clothes and swabbed his hands for gunshot residue. Now he stood waiting to hear about Alicia in borrowed clothes.

The sound of approaching footsteps had Devon stopping in his tracks. A rangy, dangerous looking man in a pair of casual slacks and a pressed shirt approached them.

Conner stood. "Hey, Carino. Thanks for coming."

"When Micah called I made sure to get the caller." He looked at Devon. "Mr. Stryker?"

Devon nodded.

"I'm Rome Carino from the HPD. I'd like to ask you a few questions."

"Okay."

"The person who is dead at the scene was Millicent Hughes?"

"Yes. She's Ali's cousin. I'm assuming that's who she is."

He nodded as he made a note. "Ali being Ms. Alicia Hughes?"

"Yes."

"Who shot her?"

"I did. She had already shot Ali, and was about to shoot her again."

Again he nodded and said nothing as he made a few notes.

"What's the damage here, Carino?" Conner asked.

He made a face. "A lot of this is out of my hands. MI-6 and CIA are all over the fucking area bagging evidence, and I get to be their liaison."

"Lucky you," Conner said.

His lips twitched before straightening out into a grim line. "Yeah. Anyway, it will be played up more than likely as a mugging. With you admitting to taking the shot, it makes it easier. You tested positive for GSR."

"Why would I lie about that?" Devon asked.

The police office shrugged. "Stupid people always do."

"I'm proud I shot the fucking bitch. In fact, if you told me she had made it to the hospital and survived, I would hunt her down and kill her again. Happily."

"Yes, well, let's keep that out of the report," Conner said.

Carino nodded. "No problem. The spooks really don't care. They'd probably like to pretend as though it didn't happen, but the noise in that area of town draws attention. Also, they're planning on trying their best to keep your name out of it."

He nodded, but he was barely paying attention now. A doctor was walking toward them.

"Mr. Stryker?"

"Yes."

"Ms. Hughes is fine. It was a flesh wound, but she hit her head, which along with the blood loss made her a little dizzy."

Relief rushed through him. "When can I see her?"

"Right now."

He didn't give either Conner or the detective a backwards glance. The doctor handed him off to a nurse, who led him back to a room. He stepped into the room and for the first time in many years, sent a prayer of thanks to the heavens. The rest of his fear seemed to thaw when he saw her. He couldn't believe how close they had come to losing her.

When he realized he was grinding his teeth, he forced himself to quit.

"Are you going to keep standing over there glaring at me?" she asked, her voice barely heard over the beeping of the machines. Her eyes were still closed, and she was as pale as the white sheets. It angered him all over again.

"If I want to."

She chuckled, then winced. He walked over to her bedside. "Are you in pain?"

"Not much. They just gave me some meds, and they are going to let me go."

"I think you should stay."

She finally opened her eyes. They were blurry with pain and meds. "I don't want to be here. The doctor said I will be fine and since I won't be alone tonight, I could go home."

He opened his mouth but the nurse came in. "I hear you're going home."

Ali nodded.

"I don't agree, but what do I know," the nurse said.

"I'm on your side," Devon murmured.

She winked at him as she started to pull out the IV. "It was only a flesh wound, but the doc did say you need to rest. I assume you will be her caregiver."

"I'll be—"

"Yes," he said interrupting Ali. He knew she was going to try and put distance between them, but he wasn't going to allow that. Not now.

"Good. Make sure she gets sleep, but not too much. If she's throwing up at all, make sure you take her to the closest ER. That could be signs of a concussion, although we don't think she has one."

He nodded.

"Excuse me, I'm right here," Ali said, her voice as petulant as a five-year-old refused a treat.

The nurse shook her head. "You let Mr. Stryker take care of you. I heard you're a mother, but you don't want to end up back here, do you? A few days of rest and you'll be all better."

Ali sighed in defeat and closed her eyes. The nurse winked at him again.

"My daughter loves your newest version of Stryker Force."

He smiled grateful she had at least gotten Ali to accept he would watch over her. "She doesn't have the newest one. It isn't out yet, but I can send her a prototype of it."

The nurse smiled. "She would love it."

He got her information and then turned to Ali. She was the one glaring at him now.

"I guess we need to get something for you to wear home. I'll get you a pair of scrubs."

He turned before she could argue with him again. He was finding out that sometimes it was just best to roll right over Ali. Otherwise, she would just argue with him until he went deaf.

Then, he stopped for a second. Home. That sounded fucking wonderful. And, once he let her rest and they sorted out the investigation, she would just have to accept it was her home too now.

ALICIA BLINKED when they turned into this driveway and found it flooded in lights. As soon as they parked, the door slammed open and Dee came running out.

"Woman, get your ass back in here," Micah yelled, as he followed her out.

The two little ones brought up the rear. Dee came around to Devon's door. As soon as he opened it, Dee jumped on him, hugging and kissing him.

Then, she smacked him. "You do that again, *I* will kill you."

Micah came over to her. He gave her an understanding smile, which was more than she'd gotten from Devon. He'd been cranky since she'd woken up in the hospital.

"How you doing, Alicia?"

"Okay."

She stepped out of the car and straightened. Her surroundings started to revolve around her again. Her stomach pitched and she stumbled a bit. With only one good arm, she almost fell.

"Whoa there," Micah said, and he grabbed her by the arm.

Devon came around the front of the car muttering all the way. Most of it was not that nice and all about her.

"Give her to me."

That autocratic tone was starting to really anger her. Why did he think he was in charge of her well-being?

"I think not," Alicia said.

Of course, Devon completely ignored her. He shoved a laughing Micah out of the way as he picked her up. Even though she knew he was angry, he was gentle with her.

"I don't need someone to carry me."

"Shut up."

"Don't tell me to shut up, wanker."

"Devon, is something wrong with Mummy?" Bridget asked. She opened her mouth to tell Bridget not to worry.

"She hit her head and her brains are a little scrambled. She also had a cut on her arm, so that's why it's in this sling. The doctor said she'll be just fine."

Bridget's frown dissolved.

"The doctor said she has to rest, so we have to make sure she does."

Her daughter trailed after them, along with Alana. "We can make sure she has lots of snacks."

Devon chuckled. "That sounds like a good thing. She also has to stay in bed."

"The doctor didn't say that."

"No, that was me. You will stay in bed."

"Will that make Mummy better?"

"Yep. She'll be all better if she stays in bed."

"That's a lie," Alicia muttered.

"Are you telling your daughter that if she feels badly she should run around getting sicker?"

Wasn't that just like the wanker to turn that around on her? She ground her teeth together.

"Good. Now, why don't you go in the kitchen with Dee while I get your mom settled in my room?"

"Okay," she said, running off with her new friend.

Devon carried her up the stairs, much like he had the day before. Had it really been only a day since they'd spent the night making love?

"Devon, you can't just order me into bed."

"I think I just did that, with the blessing of the nurse."

"You really should take me to my room."

"No."

"What?"

He stepped into his room and walked over to the bed. Alicia noticed that the bed had been made and then the sheets turned down. Devon had apparently made sure the room was prepared for them.

He set her down, again being gentle, then covered her up.

"Don't do that."

"I'll do what I want."

"It's hot, Devon. Remember, I'm accustomed to Seattle weather."

With a sigh, he shoved the sheets aside.

"There's no need to be a complete jackass, Devon."

Every muscle in his body seemed to still. "What did you say?"

"I said you're being a jackass."

He said nothing and she looked up. When she saw his face, she wished she hadn't.

Rage tightened his jaw and anger darkened his eyes. "Let me get this straight."

She opened her mouth, but he held up his hand.

"No. You will let me finish. I'm the jackass? Not you, who ran off as if you didn't have a care in the world, except for confronting your cousin."

"Yes, but—"

"No," he said, his voice a little more forceful. "You will shut up right now. You ran out there with the knowledge that the bitch might kill you. No thought to your daughter, no thought to me. You are a selfish, heartless woman, Alicia Hughes."

Then, he turned and stomped out of the room.

She stared at the empty doorway thinking he would

return, but he didn't. Her vision wavered and she realized she had started to cry. The fear, pain, and anger came rushing back to her. Her body started to shake as she sobbed. Turning onto her good side, she buried her face in the pillow and cried.

twenty-one

Devon ignored everyone in the house and strode to his office. He slammed the door behind him, not caring if it made him an ass or not. He headed straight for the whiskey on his desk. After filling the shot glass to the brim, he downed it in one long gulp. It stung as it slid down his throat and he was happy for it. Rage still poured through him as the scene in his bedroom came back to him.

She had called him a jackass. The man who had saved her from being killed, the one who loved her, father of her child...and she didn't give a damn. Rage surged and pain twisted his heart. She didn't even understand why he was so pissed or how he was feeling. And he hated to admit it, that hurt more than anything.

She didn't have the same depth of feelings.

There was a loud knock at the door. He ignored it. He wasn't in the mood for his sister agreeing with Ali or his brother-in-law telling him what he was doing wrong.

There was another loud knock and he sneered at the door as he poured another shot a whiskey and downed it. Fuck them.

Unfortunately, Sean Kaheaku was just as rude as he was. He opened the door and walked into the room. Devon shot him a dirty look.

"Want to tell me what all the yelling is about?" Kaheaku asked.

"She left."

"Yes, she did. But right now, what was all that yelling about up in the room? Bridget's a little upset."

He sighed as guilt tightened his gut further. Great, now he was pissed and he felt guilty because he had frightened his daughter.

"Do you want to know what she called me?"

"I believe she said you were acting like a jackass."

Of course he heard that. Everyone heard it. The whole entire community of Kaneohe probably heard it.

"The man who saved her."

"And you were acting like a Neanderthal."

He opened his mouth to tell Kaheaku to go fuck himself. That's when he noticed the smile.

"Don't get me wrong. If Alicia was my woman, I'd have been just as pissed. Jackass would probably be too mild of word for my behavior in that situation. I wouldn't care if she was an expert shooter—and she has been graded as such. She should have never left like that, but she wasn't thinking straight. She was trying to protect Bridget, and she was trying to protect you."

"As if I couldn't do that myself."

Kaheaku chuckled. "I'm sure if Alicia were here, she would point out that she finished her training and you didn't."

He offered Kaheaku a one finger salute.

"But I also heard her tone."

"Yeah, and what tone was that?"

"A woman in love."

Irritated, he started to pace again. "I can't believe she ran off like that."

"To confront the bitch."

"Yes. And she left me with a note," he said, motioning with his head toward the note. It was sitting on his desk, and he was still pissed about it. "Who leaves a note when they are running off to kill a woman?"

"Well, she *is* a Hughes," Kaheaku murmured, as he picked up the note.

"What the bloody hell does that mean?"

The other man looked up, a smile curving his lips. "Now you sound like Alicia. And for the meaning, the family is legendary for putting country before their own safety."

"Well, I think that legend can be put to death," he said, tossing back the rest of his whiskey. "Millicent took care of that."

"No one will ever hear about that, you know? The family will have a reputation that is as sterling as the queen's silver."

"Thanks to Ali."

"Partially, but don't think this has anything to do with the reputation of her family. Her running off like that was because she had some kind of stupid idea of protecting you and in turn, protecting Bridget."

Devon collapsed in his chair. "I am so fucking sick of all the riddles. It was why I was never going to be good in the CIA. I like to play with puzzles, but I need facts in my personal life."

Kaheaku was apparently in the mood to take pity on him. "She left you this before she went to kill Millicent?"

He nodded. "Just leaves. Tells me to take care of our daughter and walks away."

"You're a dumbass. So dumb, that I can't believe I'm going to help you."

"What the hell do you mean?"

Sean sighed. "You didn't last in the Company, so you might not understand what this means. For someone like Alicia, this is..."

"What?"

"A lot of us don't have a family like the Hughes. The UK has more of them in the business basically because many of them, like the Hughes, date back several hundred years. They have been serving God and country from the moment they are born. It's expected of them, bred into the bones in a way. But being in the business like this makes you very close knit. I never saw anyone who cared more about his family than her father. He adored her. With the death of his wife, Walter became fanatical, a bit warped. He obsessed about Alicia's safety."

"So, he pulls her into the business?" Devon snorted. "Talk about warped."

"With years of service, no matter what Walter did, Alicia was always going to be in some kind of danger. It wasn't as bad as he probably thought it was, but dangerous all the same. The one thing he left her was her ability to fight off any attack. He also taught her to be a bit autocratic. She truly believed she was better at handling the situation than you were. So, just as her father had taught her, she took charge."

He closed his eyes and tried not to see Millicent standing there with her gun trained on Alicia. When he opened his eyes, Devon found Sean giving him a sympathetic look.

"And almost got herself killed in the process."

"Yep. Just like he did all those years ago when he started searching for the traitor. When he found out it was the niece he had helped raise, it was probably a big blow. Instead of turning her in, I bet he had set some meeting with her to get her to surrender. It's probably why she killed him."

"And she was within seconds of killing Ali."

"That close?"

He swallowed trying to force the bile down. "She had a gun pointed at her and was ready to shoot again when I shot her."

Sean shook his head. "That girl was always pushing the envelope. Like when she went looking for you without an assignment."

"I can't complain about that one."

Sean chuckled. "Of course. But, you aren't looking closely enough at this letter. Spies give away a lot of things. They give people their money, their peace of mind...even their souls to get the job done. We hardly ever give our trust."

"Yeah?"

"Fuck, for being a genius, you are damned stupid."

Devon continued to study Kaheaku wondering if he could take the man. He was pissing him off and right now,

Devon needed to expend that anger. Knowing Kaheaku's background, there was a good chance Devon would get his ass kicked instead.

"Well, shit, Stryker. You're in love with her. Can't you figure it out? For someone in our business, trusting is harder than loving. She *trusts* you. Naming you as the father of her child and leaving Bridget in your care shows just how much she does trust you. Probably the first person in a really long time. Don't fuck it up, or you might just leave her completely lost to men."

Kaheaku didn't wait for a response. Instead, he turned and walked away, leaving Devon alone to his thoughts. Just outside of the door his family milled. He knew that Dee was ready to know everything and right now. She never had much patience when it came to things like that. And, he could call Micah his family. He knew that no matter what, he could trust the man.

And then there was Bridget. The daughter he hadn't known a couple weeks ago. After the last few days, he couldn't think of living a life without her or her mother in it.

Ali. The woman made him insane. He did all kinds of things the wrong way when she was around. He slept with a woman he barely knew that night in Vegas. Just a few days, and he knew her inside and out. A backbone of steel and an attitude to go with it, hid a vulnerability that touched something deep inside of him he thought he'd lost. She made him so damned angry, but one look from her and his knees when weak.

And he didn't want to live without her.

He stood and went over to the wall safe behind the

books. He moved them aside and opened it. There were papers sitting inside of it, important things like a will and the trust fund he set up for Alana—that one was a secret because Micah would be pissed. He pushed those aside and found the velvet ring box. He pulled it out and opened it.

Sparkling there in the middle of red satin was his grandmother's engagement ring. She had left it to him with a note that he was to stop planning life and live it. Even all those years ago, his grandmother knew him. Thankfully, his mother had hidden it from his father or he probably would have never gotten it.

Devon drew in a deep breath and closed the box. The decision was definitely made and he wasn't going to take no for an answer.

THIRTY MINUTES LATER, Alicia still didn't have her emotions under control. She knew it all didn't have to do with what went on between Devon and her.

No, this was a cathartic release she needed. Since her father's death, her life had spiraled out of control. She had held it together for herself, then for Bridget. She'd played the good spy. Knowing that the girl she played with growing up had caused all this pain was a bit too much to take—even for a master spy's daughter.

She held her daughter close to her chest as she continued to cry.

"Why are you so sad, Mummy?" Bridget asked her.

Embarrassment heated her face. She wiped away the tears. "Oh, just a little sad, that's all. I lost a friend today and I found out she wasn't too nice."

She had never cried in front of her daughter, not once. The argument with Devon had pushed her over the edge, and she'd lost the fight with her tears.

"Was Devon angry with me? Did I do something wrong?"

The fear of disappointing Devon was easy to hear in her voice. She pulled back and looked at her daughter. She knew Devon would never do anything to hurt her.

"Oh, poppet, no. You didn't do anything wrong. Devon and Mummy had a fight."

"Oh."

Bridget didn't understand. She was really too young to pick up on what the undercurrents meant. With just the two of them for all of her life, Bridget didn't understand arguments. She sighed and slipped her hand over her daughter's golden hair. She had important things to discuss, and she wasn't quite sure how to approach it. Alicia was a woman who planned for everything, but this had never been on her horizon. Not until she decided to have a fun Saturday at the market.

"How do you like Devon?"

Bridget smiled. "He's nice when he doesn't frown. He has a nice smile."

"That's true. He does have a very nice smile."

"His eyes are like Dee's. But, they're twins."

She drew in a deep breath, and slowly released it. "Yes, they are."

"And they're like mine. I have eyes like theirs."

Leave it up to her daughter to pick up on that. Four years old. She shook her head. Her father had said Alicia had been a precocious child, solving puzzles on a teenage level when she was barely seven. She should have known with a father like Devon that Bridget would turn out even smarter.

"Yes, you both have the same eyes. Do you know why?"

Bridget shook her head.

"That's because, a long time ago, Devon and I knew each other."

"You knew him before I was born?"

Alicia nodded and decided to take the plunge. "He's your daddy."

Bridget didn't react right away. Alicia knew her daughter and knew she was putting the pieces together in her mind, trying to understand the situation.

"What do you think about that?" Alicia finally asked.

"Does that mean Alana is my cousin?"

Alicia nodded. "And Dee's your aunt and Micah is your uncle. What do you think about that?" she asked again.

Bridget smiled. "That's okay, but I don't want to live here. I want to move back to Washington."

"I'm sure we can figure something out," Alicia said.

"Hey, do you think Devon would come live with us? He can stay in the guest room. I think he's lonely."

Fresh tears burned the backs of her eyes. "Why do you say that?"

Bridget shrugged. "You said you were lonely until you had me. Now he doesn't have to be lonely."

She noticed a movement out of the corner of her eye and

saw Devon standing there. His hands were in his pockets, his eyes filled with a vulnerability she had never seen.

"I'll see what he says. Why don't you go play with Alana before she has to head home?"

She leaned forward and kissed Bridget's forehead. She scrambled off the bed and hurried out of the room. Devon stopped her before she left the room and whispered in her ear. Bridget looked back at Alicia, then she looked at Devon and nodded.

She skipped out of the room.

"Where have you been?" she asked, trying to keep things light. What the bloody hell did she say now?

"In my office, drinking."

"Well, that's good."

He smiled at her sarcasm and walked into the room. "I had a talk with Kaheaku. He seems to think that I'm a dumbass."

She shrugged and instantly regretted it. Pain flashed in her arm and then filtered down to her hand. Dammit.

"And I have to agree."

She frowned. "What are you talking about Devon?"

He sat on the bed where her daughter had been and took her free hand in his. "There are times when we were growing up that Dee would tell me I was too smart for my own good. And I'll admit it to you and no one else, she was right."

She was tired and in immense pain. She just didn't have the patience to banter back and forth. For some reason, she felt the need to cry again, but she was strong enough to fight it for the moment.

"You're talking in riddles."

"Now you know how it feels." He pulled out the note she wrote. "You gave her to me and told me to keep her safe."

"I know what I put in the note."

"I get a lot of things. It's weird being this rich and have people give you things. Some of the things are worth thousands."

"How nice for you," she said.

His lips curved. "But nothing, not anything I can buy and not anything I am given, is worth more to me than what you gave me."

The happy tears she had held back just a few seconds earlier spilled down her cheeks. He wiped them away.

"From the time I saw you sitting at my favorite table in Vegas, you've had a hold on me. And now...I want you in my life. I want both of you with me, always. I was so pissed when you left earlier, you want to know why?"

She shook her head.

"Now that I have you with me, I don't ever want you to go away. It scared the hell out of me just how much you had come to mean to me. And now, there's Bridget in the mix...I love you both so much. Please, don't ever do that again."

She sighed then closed her eyes. The emotions of that moment, of knowing she had to risk everything to gain what she needed, came rushing back to her. She opened her eyes. "I needed to know she would have someone there for her. She deserved to have someone who loved her more than themselves. I knew you would."

"And you picked me. You could have picked someone else, like Dee."

"Well, you're her father and don't think I didn't see how you felt about her. It was so easy to see in your eyes."

He swallowed and reached into his pocket again. "Then, I am going to hold you to all of this, and use your vulnerability right now to my advantage."

He held out a small black box, which he opened. Snuggled securely in the red satin sat a ring. It was set on top of a white gold band.

"It was my grandmother's ring. I've had it for a few years now, and somewhere in the back of my mind, I knew it was yours."

She said nothing. She couldn't. A lump now clogged her throat, and it seemed all the air had backed up in her lungs.

"Ali?" She looked up at him. "Marry me. Let's be a family."

She swallowed as happiness bloomed inside her heart. "Oh, Devon, yes, I'll marry you."

Relief softened his eyes. He pulled out the ring and carefully slipped it on her finger.

"But there is one rule."

"What's that?" he asked.

"Bridget said we need to go back to Seattle. Oh, and you can stay in the guest room."

He laughed. "I'll have a chat with her about that guest room."

She was laughing when he bent his head to kiss

epilogue

Alicia looked out over the wedding guests milling around the ballroom at the casino hotel. Satisfaction and happiness danced through her. Alana and Bridget were running around, stealing bits of cake and giggling while they did it. Her new sister-in-law laughed at their antics. Dee was standing next to her friend May. The gorgeous Hawaiian held her newborn son.

The entire management of Rough 'n Ready came over for the wedding. She knew it was expensive for them to do, but Micah and Evan had closed down the club, citing a family gathering. And, looking at the way everyone was interacting, Alicia realized it was true. While not all blood related, this was a family.

Six months ago, Alicia would have never thought this would be her. Not only had she gained a husband, but also a wealth of friends that included two BDSM club owners, a former FBI agent and somewhere along the way, an Australian cowboy. One top of it, she reconnected with Sean.

She looked down at her ring. She had her life back. No, she had a better life and all because of one man. As if he read her mind, Strong arms slipped around her waist.

"Well, Mrs. Stryker, we do know how to throw a wedding," Devon said as he nibbled on her earlobe.

She patted his hand and turned to face him. "We do. A bloody amazing wedding. You don't think it's tacky we had it in Las Vegas, do you?"

He shook his head as a sexy smile curved his lips. "No. It's where I fell in love with you."

Her heart squeezed tight, but she rolled her eyes. She still wasn't accustomed to the way Devon expressed himself. It had to be the Italian in him. The man never seemed to have an issue with telling her how he felt. She lived for each and every comment, but Alicia still had to come to terms with it.

"No, it's true. Couldn't get you out of my mind," he said as he slid his hands up to cup her face. "You captured me that night, love. My heart and my soul."

Alicia lifted her hands and slid her fingers around his wrists. "You don't have to keep saying things like that."

"But I want to."

She smiled and leaned up to give him a kiss. Just a simple brush of her mouth had her body humming. When she pulled back, Devon kept his eyes closed for a few seconds before slowly opening them.

"You kiss me like that and I have to behave? Doesn't seem fair."

She opened her mouth to retort his question, but she spotted Sean heading to the door.

"I need to catch him."

Devon nodded and kissed her nose. She hurried through the crowd and caught Sean right before he reached the door.

"Leaving without dancing with the bride, Sean?"

He turned and smiled. "I walked you down the aisle. I don't need a dance."

She took his hand and walked with him out into the corridor. "That's rude."

He chuckled then faced her. She still didn't like what she saw there. He'd disappeared after her adventure, returning with a few more scrapes and bruises than before he left. Sean would never talk about it, she knew, but something went horribly wrong on the last mission.

"I never said I was nice."

"But you are, and I know it."

He studied her for a long moment. "I'm glad you're happy."

The simple statement meant more to her than any well wishes from anyone else. "You think Father would approve?"

"Yes. But not because of any reason other than you love Stryker and he is stupid in love with you. It was what your father would have wanted for you."

She shook her head as her eyes filled.

"Good God, don't start doing *that* again," Sean said, his voice filled with enough panic she started to laugh. He'd threatened to leave when she cried before the wedding. She couldn't help it. She saw Bridget in her little flower girl dress and lost it.

"Sorry. It's just so sweet. Big bad spy Sean Kaheaku is afraid of women's tears."

He jerked a shoulder and looked around as if to make sure no one heard her calling him sweet.

"Don't worry. Your secret is safe with me, Sean."

He continued to look around and she knew that he was running out on her reception to go to a job. He'd postponed it for her, but Sean needed the work. Not for the money, but Sean needed to keep busy. She knew he did it to keep from dealing with real life.

Alicia couldn't judge him on that one.

"Where are you running to this time?"

"I have a job."

"With Lassiter."

She didn't need to ask. She knew from the expression on his face. And she knew he wouldn't tell her where he was going.

"I have a plane waiting for me."

Anxiety pushed away some of her happiness. She had a really bad feeling about this. "Please, be careful. I don't trust him or your companions on this matter."

"I'm going solo."

That alarmed her even more. Going on an assignment into hostile area was considered suicidal.

"Don't look like that. I can handle it."

"Going in by yourself is not a good idea. You know exactly what they'll say about you."

He shoved a hand through his hair. "I don't really give a fuck what they think."

"Then why are you doing it?"

"You did it when you went after Stryker."

"I was desperate. And it was the wrong place to go after

him. My father would have had my head on a platter if he had known I was doing that. And he would say the same thing about this."

"So you know better than I do?"

She shook her head. "Answer me this. Would you have tried to talk me out of going to Vegas?"

"Would it have worked?"

Of course it wouldn't have. "That was different."

"How?"

"My father was involved. What has you running away to God knows where?"

He looked away for a moment, then back at her. "I just have to do it. I have to do something."

She wanted to say more—so much more. But she knew better. She would never convince him to stay.

"Promise me you will be safe?"

"Always." He leaned close to her and gave her a kiss on the cheek. "Be happy, Alicia. You both deserve it."

Then, he turned and walked away from her. Helplessly, Alicia watched him walk down the hallway. She felt Devon's approach before he touched her. She leaned her head on his shoulder as he slipped an arm around her waist.

"You're worried about him."

"I know where he is, mentally."

He kissed her temple. "You were never there, were you?"

"Close, for different reasons."

"When?"

"Twice. When I came looking for you, then after my father was killed and I had to go on the run. I'm not sure what I would have done if I hadn't been pregnant for Bridget. Knowing I was the only person in the world for her, I had to be careful. Sean doesn't have that."

He turned her around to face him. "Well, now you have two of us to take care of."

She smiled and slipped her arms up over his shoulders. "Is that a fact?"

"Uh-uh."

He bent his head and kissed her. This time it wasn't as sweet as before. His tongue slipped between her lips and into her mouth. Her blood heated, her head started to spin.

She pushed him back. "Stop that. We have a room full of guests."

"Screw them."

She giggled.

"God, I love that sound," he said and gave her another hard, quick kiss. "I talked to Dee. They will handle Bridget and we spent over an hour in there. We have permission to disappear."

"Is that true?"

"Yes," he said, grabbing her hand and tugging her toward the elevator. As soon as the doors opened, he pulled her into the car and used his card to gain access to the penthouse.

"And, I am very happy you decided to not to wear a bunch of skirts beneath this dress."

"Is that a fact?" she asked. Before she finished asking, though, he had squatted in front of her. Without saying a word, he shoved her dress up. He leaned in and the moment before he touched her, she felt his breath. She knew she should stop him. They were in public and there were probably cameras, but the moment she felt his mouth on her bare flesh, she stopped thinking.

He slipped his tongue inside of her, lapping at her, teasing her clit to the point that she was ready to come. But, the door dinged and opened to the penthouse.

Devon pulled back and dragged her into the suite.

"I should take my time with you," he said, as he unzipped his pants.

"You can do that. Later," she said, kissing his throat as he lifted her up and stumbled over to the wall. He positioned her there and thrust into her. She almost came right there and then. She was dripping wet, her need building to new heights each time he plunged into her pussy.

He kissed her throat, her mouth. She sucked on his tongue and moaned as her orgasm washed over her. He shouted her name as he drove himself into her once more before giving over to the pleasure.

Moments later, he stumbled backwards, falling onto the couch in the living area. He grunted as he took the brunt of her weight.

"Sorry, that wasn't that romantic of a beginning to a wedding night," he mumbled.

She lifted her head. "I can't think of a more brilliant way to start a wedding night."

He opened his eyes. "Is that a fact?"

She nodded. "My husband stole me away from the reception because he couldn't keep his hands off of me. I find that to be the most romantic way to start a wedding night."

He brushed her hair away from her face. "I can promise you that I will never be able to keep my hands off you, love."

She smiled then settled against him, her head on his shoulder and her hand over his heart. Definitely the best way to start a wedding night...and the rest of their lives.

THANK you so much for reading Harmless Secrets! If you want to read Dee and Micah's story, check out *A Little Harmless Lie*!

If you are a fan of the intense, growly, "don't even look at my woman" hero, Micah is definitely for you. The fun he has showing her the BDSM lifestyle is super hot. Dee has just enough spunk to not always listen to her Dom 100% of the time. And Micah loves every second of it.

—*SMEXY BOOKS*

Buy today-> A Little Harmless Lie

harmless revenge

Sean's story is coming up in August!

Buy the book | Read an Excerpt

He thinks he's on his own.

Sean Kaheaku always been a man on top of his game. And that game is international espionage. Not on the bad end of it. He's one of the good guys. Or he had been until about six months ago. His whole world got turned upside down and he's still trying to figure out what to do about it. So, he went home to Hawaii, and that's exactly where he is, trying to figure out what to do now that he's been burned as a security agent.

But when two of his old lovers arrive in Honolulu, **Jaime Alexander** and **Randy Young** won't leave him alone. He refuses their help and they ignore him. As they spend time together, old feelings float to the surface, and the twosome becomes a threesome. Their nights together are hotter than even the Hawaiian sun. It's exciting and overwhelming at the same time, and it starts to feel as if this could be something special.

But even as their threesome starts to feel as if it will last more than just a few weeks, danger arrives at their doorstep, intent on destroying everything Sean loves–including Randy and Jaime.

»**WARNING: This book contains three spies who like to play games in and out of the bedroom, hot m/m loving, more m/m/f loving, dangerous games, lies, a few misdemeanors, and love scenes so hot, even most Addicts will be shocked. There is also a group of Alpha males with badges who will have their own series, a heroine who knows how to handle her two men, and two men who know exactly what she likes. As usual, ice and towels should be handy to help you through the book.**

tfh team bravo

Coming this October, a new chapter in the Task Force Hawaii Saga!

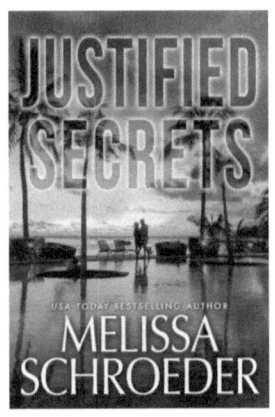

PREORDER TODAY

Everyone has secrets, but hers could get them both killed.

Autumn Bradford has always been a little...different. The daughter of a cult leader, she has spent her life fighting the bad guys and searching for the father everyone thinks is dead. One thing stands in her way, the new leader of Team Bravo. Former SEAL Seth Harrington accepted the job at TFH for a new start. Years of dangerous missions has left his body and soul scarred. He doesn't have time for a woman with too many secrets and the eating habits of a hobbit-no matter how attractive he finds her.

Autumn doesn't need a keeper or a protector, but every time she turns around, Seth seems to be there. Time together makes it difficult to avoid their attraction, and one stolen kiss makes it impossible to resist the temptation. Falling in love wasn't in the plans for either of them, but Seth realizes he will do anything to protect her, even if it means facing down the most dangerous man either of them know: her father.

Author Note: This is a Harmless World Novel with our favorite crime fighting heroes and heroines! There are secrets (duh!), inappropriate jokes, Hawaiian food, a betting pool as usual, a new team to get to know, and a training session that goes a little too far.

Meet the new team of Task Force Hawaii. Lead by former SEAL Seth Harrington, they focus on search and rescue, but also support Team Alpha.

Each member of TEAM Bravo will be pushed to the brink as

they start their duty as the main search and rescue division of Task Force Hawaii.

TEAM MEMBERS
Captain: Seth Harrington
Ryan Morrison w/ rescue dog Maya
Nikki Kekoa
Robbie Ramirez
Kapone Hanson (Kap)

about the author

From an early age, USA Today Best-selling author Melissa loved to read. When she discovered the romance genre, she started to listen to the voices in her head. After years of following her AF Major husband around, she is happy to be settled in Northern Virginia surrounded by horses, wineries, and many, many Wegmans.

Keep up with Mel, her releases, and her appearances by subscribing to her <u>NEWSLETTER</u>. If you want to keep up with cover reveals, new behind the scene info on her writing, and when new excerpts are posted, follow her MelissaSchroeder.net News News. Or you can do both! They are low traffic, so you will not get tons of emails.

Check out all her other books, family trees and other info at <u>her website!</u>
<u>If you would want contact Mel, email her at: melissa@ melissaschroeder.net</u>

instagram.com/melschro

amazon.com/author/melissa_schroeder

facebook.com/MelissaSchroederfanpage

bookbub.com/authors/melissa-schroeder

goodreads.com/Melissa_Schroeder

tiktok.com/@melissawritesromance

www.ingramcontent.com/pod-product-compliance
Lightning Source LLC
Chambersburg PA
CBHW052041240626
47153CB00006B/2187